Star Child

Distributed in Canada by H. B. Fenn and Company Ltd.

Library of Congress Cataloging-in-Publication Data
has been applied for.

ISBN: 978-0-7534-6205-8

Kingfisher books are available for special promotions and premiums.
For details contact: Director of Special Markets, Holtzbrinck Publishers.

First American Edition September 2008
Printed in India
1 3 5 7 9 8 6 4 2
1TR/0208/THOM/SC/80STORA/C

Zodiac Girls

Star Child

Cathy Hopkins

KINGFISHER
NEW YORK

Chapter One

Zodiac Girl

<u>Thebe's list of things to do</u>
1) Look up this month's (May) horoscope on the Internet.
2) Do homework.
3) Set out clothes for school.
4) Do grocery shopping online.
5) Leave list of things to do for Mrs. Watson, housekeeper.
6) Practice ice-skating.

"Omigiddyaunt!" I said to our black cat, Cosmo, who looked up with sleepy eyes from the end of my bed. "This is *so* fantastic."

I was sitting at my desk, and I went back to the website that I'd been looking at on my computer to double-check that I hadn't dreamed what I'd seen. Actually, it was my dad's website: www.battyestars.org. Dad being Benjamin Battye, a celebrity astrologer. He writes a weekly column for the *Sunday Times* newspaper, a monthly column in *Divine Divas*, a glossy designer magazine, and he's on TV every Friday on "Good Morning America" talking about what's up and coming in the sky for the weekend and discussing a chosen celebrity's horoscope each month. I couldn't wait to share my news with him. I got up and raced to the top of the stairs.

"Dad. Da-*ad*!"

"What is it, munchkin?" Dad called from somewhere on the first floor.

"I think it's going to be me this month."

"I said it might be, didn't I? Come on down and we'll double-check on my computer and see what's next."

I took a quick glance in the mirror at the end of the hall. A small 13-year-old girl with brown eyes, coffee-colored skin, and braided hair looked back at me. "Today's going to be your day," I said to my reflection, and then I took the stairs down two at a time and clomped along the wooden floor to find him. This was the best thing that could ever happen, and it was happening to me. *Me*. Thebe Battye.

I'd just seen it written in my horoscope on the computer. Planetary lineups like that only happen once in a lifetime and sometimes not at all for some people. I was so happy—I felt like doing a cartwheel. Usually if anything exciting happened it was to someone else in my family. They're all so glamorous, swanning around living extraordinary lives, being the center of attention, and I'm usually there in the background being Little Miss Boring to whom nothing ever happens.

My mom's famous, too. She didn't used to be when we (me and my older sister, Pat) were younger. She was a stay-at-home mom then, but around five years ago she signed up to do a business degree at a nearby university and discovered that she had a talent for making money. She lost 40 pounds, got herself some hair extensions—so instead of her hair being short and frizzy, it was suddenly shoulder length and sleek—and then she went out and bought a new closet full of clothes. It was a case of "Watch out world, here comes Estella Battye, businesswoman supreme and a force to be reckoned with!"

Dad says it's because she is an Aries and Aries is ruled by the planet Mars, which is the planet of war! It's true—Mom is not someone to mess with when she has a project going on! Now she runs Battye Enterprises, which deals with everything and anything having to do with astrology. All aspects. You name it—she sources it and then sells it: mugs, T-shirts, necklaces, rings, books, cards, key chains, personalized horoscopes written by Dad. He had always been famous, but Mom made him *rich* and famous. When she started raking in the megabucks, she bought us a bigger house and named it Zodiac Lodge. It's near Osbury, which is a town built on a sacred site. Legend has it that it was a home of the ancient gods and twinned with Mount Olympus in Greece. All of the rooms are decorated with an astrological theme. For example, the bathroom is the Pisces room, as that's the sign of the fish as well as being a water sign, and Pisces is ruled by the planet Neptune, and Neptune is known as the king of the sea—so the bathroom has a strong marine theme. It's blue and green with pictures of fish and mermaids and a border around the top with shells on it. Very pretty. The décor of the whole house was done that way—each room with its own theme according to the stars. My best friend, Rachel, loves coming here and looking at all of the rooms. She says it's like visiting a colorful art gallery.

I almost collided with Pat, who came out of the kitchen holding a glass of juice. "Whoa, slow down. What's the hurry?" she said.

"Me. I think I'm a Zodiac Girl this month. Isn't that fantastic?"

Pat shrugged. "If you say so," she said and sauntered on. Pat isn't interested in astrology at all. Mom and Dad named her Mahina when she was born. She was born under the sign of Cancer, and Cancerians are ruled by the Moon. *Mahina* means "the moon," and I think it's a lovely, romantic name. Not my sister, though. When she was nine, she demanded that no one call her that anymore, and she changed her name to Pat. *Pat!* She doesn't look like a Pat. She looks like a Mahina. She's very pretty, with big brown eyes, a heart-shaped face, and black hair (extensions, like Mom) halfway down her back.

Her room on the top floor is the only one that doesn't have a zodiac theme—at least not anymore. It is decorated to reflect the Moon and has a navy ceiling covered in teeny lights that twinkle like stars. Sleeping in there is like being outside on a cloudless night, plus there's a skylight, so part of what you can see is the real sky. When Pat was ten, she threw away all of the star posters and the moon-shaped lamp and painted the room white, even the ceiling. On her door she put a poster saying, "KEEP OUT OR RISK PAIN OF DEATH. STRICTLY NO ZODIAC STUFF IN HERE. ALSO RISK PAIN OF DEATH." And then she added a skull and crossbones to emphasize that she was serious. Dad says she reacts like that because she has the Moon in Scorpio and being cynical about things like horoscopes is typical of someone with a birth chart like hers. She's one of the most popular girls at our school. She's 16, and there's a long line of boys vying for her attention. She usually breaks their hearts, though, simply because she can.

I found Dad stretched out in his study at the back of the house. Dad liked to dress as if he was still in the Caribbean (which is where our family is originally from, although Pat and I were born in the United States). He was wearing one of his brightly colored Hawaiian shirts with red parrots on it, long shorts, and sandals. With his shoulder-length dreadlocks, he looked like a reggae musician. Mom and he do look funny together, like she's Mrs. Straight and he's Mr. Chilled Out.

The study is the room that has been themed around the planet Mercury, which is the planet of communication. Also, Mercury was known in the time of the Greek gods as the winged messenger. Mercury is the ruling planet for both Gemini and Virgo. Dad is a Gemini and I am a Virgo, so we have the Mercury connection in common. Dad thought it was appropriate to have his study be the Mercury room, as that's where he does all of his communicating—through his computer and his phone—and all of his books are in there. Loads of them. Some of them are ancient, with worn, leather covers and faded paper inside, and the words are written in beautiful handwriting. It's a large, cool room with high ceilings and French windows that open out onto the backyard when the weather's warm. Dad has two old leather sofas in front of a marble fireplace, where he likes to lie down and read. He sometimes reads five or six books at a time, and he leaves them open all over the place, so I often trip over them. On the walls are some paintings he got in India, and they depict the various planets in astrology. In the corner near the desk he has a life-size bronze statue of Mercury that one of his Hollywood clients bought him as a thank-you gift. I personally think it's a little risqué, as the statue is totally nude, and sometimes when you sit on the sofa, its you-know-what is at eye level. Not exactly what I want to be looking at when I'm in there having a little chat with Dad, thank you very much. I put a yellow Post-it note on it once to cover up the not-so-private private parts. Dad thought it was hysterically funny and called in the whole family to look. I had never been so embarrassed in my entire life. I find it annoying being in Dad's study sometimes because it's so messy and I am dying to clean it up, but he won't let me touch a thing.

"It's my room," he says, "and I have my own system." It's weird—Virgos and Geminis might have the same ruling planet, but as signs go, they are sooooo different. Virgos like things neat.

"Here, take a look at this," said Dad, and he beckoned me over to a shelf, where he heaved down one of his ancient books. When it thudded onto his desk, a cloud of dust blew up and made me sneeze.

"A-CHOOOOOOO! Honestly, Dad, one day I'm going to sneak in here with a feather duster and a mask and clean this place from top to bottom!"

"I dare you. I like it like this. It's lived in."

"A-CHOOOOOOOOOOOOOOOO!" I sneezed again.

Dad ignored me and kept on turning pages. "Ah, here we are," he said. "I knew it was in here somewhere."

I glanced down at the page he had opened the book to. The words *Zodiac Girls* were written in large, old-fashioned letters and were illustrated in different-colored inks with a night sky behind them.

"Let's see what it says," said Dad, and he leaned in to study the page closer. "Hmm, yes, yes, ruling planets, we know all about that. The planets are here in human form. Yes, yes . . ."

I had seen this chapter ages ago because I loved to go through Dad's books, especially the older ones. I liked the sense of history in them, the feeling that someone in some ancient time, before the days of spell checkers and copy and paste, had sat down and written every word and even illustrated some of them. I remembered reading that there were such people as Zodiac Girls, but I hadn't paid too much attention, until recently when Dad had said that he suspected I might be one.

I leaned over his shoulder and read. "Zodiac Girls. Somewhere on Earth, every month, one maiden is chosen to be a Zodiac Girl. This entitles her to:

1) A gift of jewelry to wear that is appropriate to her sign.

2) A means of communicating with the planets.

3) The assistance of the planets, who are all here on Earth in disguise as normal people.

4) The ruling planet of each sign will act as a guardian for one month only."

Awesome, I thought as I glanced down at the list of signs and their ruling planets.

Ruling planet	Sign
Sun	Leo
Moon	Cancer
Mercury	Gemini and Virgo
Venus	Taurus and Libra
Mars	Aries
Jupiter	Sagittarius
Saturn	Capricorn
Uranus	Aquarius
Neptune	Pisces
Pluto	Scorpio

"You know the part about the planets being here in human form?" I asked.

"Yes."

"What will Mercury be here as?"

Dad looked at the book. "Hmm, Mercury, the winged messenger. Well, your guess is as good as mine." He flipped the page over. "See, this book is centuries old, so how he appears may change from age to age. He would have had something to do with messages and communication, though, I would imagine. How that manifests today, no doubt we'll find out." Dad pointed at a birth chart on the right-hand side of the page. "But look here. This is the chart of a typical Zodiac Girl showing how the planetary lineup will look when it's her month as a Zodiac Girl."

I glanced down at the page and saw the birth chart there. To someone who didn't know, it would just look like a circle with a smaller circle inside it and lines drawn across it. To me, though—I knew at a glance what most of it meant. I'd watched Dad figure out birth charts for his clients just about every day of my life. I'd never known a home that lived and breathed astrology as much as ours. Like, most babies had crib mobiles with ducks or teddy bears or fish on them, but I had had a mobile with the planets hanging from it. By the time I was five, I knew the stars as well as I knew the alphabet. I also knew that there was more to astrology than the horoscopes in magazines and newspapers. I knew that each and every person's horoscope was different, depending on what time and where he or she was born and where the planets were in the sky in relation to that. It was a real science, not hocus-pocus, as some of Dad's critics claimed.

"Now, quick," said Dad, "print out the planetary lineup for your chart this month. I've got it up on the screen now."

I went over to the computer, pressed the print

button, and a second later the sheet of paper was in my hand. I took it over to Dad, who placed it on the left-hand side of the page of the book. We looked at the chart in the book and then at mine.

"Bingo," said Dad.

"Bingo," I replied.

They matched each other perfectly. Same lineup.

Just at that moment, there was a knock at the front door. We heard Pat go to open it, and then a moment later there was the muffled sound of voices. Soon after, there were footsteps in the corridor, and Pat opened the study door. She looked bright eyed and flushed. "Um, Thebe. Someone's here for you."

"Who is it?"

"Some motorcycle messenger," she said, and then she lowered her voice and whispered, "and he's a *total* babe, like a Greek god in a leather jacket."

A tingle of excitement went through me. I smiled at Dad, and he winked back at me. "Oh, I think we might know exactly who it is," I said. "Um . . . tell him to come in. We've been expecting him."

Chapter Two

Hermie

"Welcome," said Dad, doing an awkward type of bow-curtsy, as if he wasn't sure how to behave with a six-foot-tall motorcycle messenger in his study. The stranger appeared just as unsure and looked around at the paintings and books in amazement. He was just as Pat had described him, around 18, maybe older, but a total babe with a handsome face, chiseled jaw, and tall, broad-shouldered body. He reminded me of the statues of the Greek and Roman gods that we'd seen at the Metropolitan Museum of Art when we went there on a school trip—too good looking to be true, and yet here he was standing in front of us radiating health and charisma. I had a feeling that I was staring at him open mouthed, and I made a conscious effort to close my jaw. Not that he noticed. He had seen the statue of Mercury and was staring at it in surprise. It did resemble him, and I wondered how he felt about finding a statue of himself with no clothes on in my dad's study.

"It's Mercury," said Dad with a glance at the statue, "and I'm Benjamin Battye."

"And I'm Hermes, but you can call me Hermie," said the messenger boy.

"Isn't *Hermes* the Greek name for the god of travel and communication?" asked Dad with a sly wink at me. "And *Mercury* is the Roman name for the same god?"

Hermie looked impressed. "Hmm, you know your gods," he replied and then opened his jacket to reveal a T-shirt underneath with the words *Mercury Communications* written on it.

"And I know my planets," said Dad with another wink.

"Really?" asked Hermie.

Dad nodded, tapped his nose, and indicated the paintings and posters on the wall and the books on his shelves. Hermie took a closer look at some of the titles, while I desperately tried to think of something to say, but my brain seemed to have turned to mush, and all I could do was stare.

Dad pointed at the ancient book that was still open to the chapter about Zodiac Girls. "See this, Hermie?"

Hermie glanced over and looked even more impressed. "Remarkable. Absolutely remarkable. So . . . you know about us?"

Dad nodded, and Hermie's face lit up.

"I must tell the others. It's amazing. Usually we meet with such resistance, suspicion. People think we're delusional or living in a fantasyland."

"Not here in Osbury, you won't," said Dad. "We know the legends about this place and were hoping that you'd be back someday. I hope that you'll consider Zodiac Lodge to be your second home. We are honored to have you here."

Hermie looked surprised but delighted. "It is rare to find such a welcome, so that's very kind of you, sir. Most kind."

All this time, I'd been waiting for Hermie to notice *me*. I was a Zodiac Girl after all, not Dad, and at last Hermie turned away from his fascination with Dad's bookshelves, pulled a package out of the inside pocket of his jacket, and looked at me. "Am I right in thinking that you are Miss Thebe Battye?"

I could hardly breathe. "Yes. That's me," I whispered.

He handed me a box. "Then this is for you."

I felt myself blush as I took the package and was about to open it when there was a commotion in the hall, and moments later the door opened and Mom burst in looking her usual elegant self in a navy suit, filling the room with the scent of her expensive French perfume. She took one look at Hermie and her face broke into a wide grin, showing her gleaming white teeth (she'd had them whitened last month by a top cosmetic dentist). "Oh Lord. You're here! And *so* handsome."

"Estella, this is Hermie," said Dad. "And Hermie,

this is my wife, Estella."

Mom shook her head from side to side. She was still beaming. "Benjamin thought it might be today. I got back as soon as I could. Oh Lord, but this is *exciting*. Isn't this exciting, Thebe?" she asked without even glancing at me. She couldn't take her eyes off Hermie. "Now, Hermie, honey. You know who we are? What we do? Did Benjamin explain?"

"Um . . . I'm starting to get an idea," said Hermie with a grin.

"Battye's the name, astrology's our game," said Mom, and she did a little skipping dance. "Oo-ee, I can't resist a moment longer. I have to give you a hug." She went over and embraced Hermie, who didn't seem to mind at all. "Welcome. Welcome here. Benjamin, have you given him a guided tour of the house?"

Dad shook his head. "He only just got here a few seconds ago, Estella."

"Have you been offered some refreshments, Hermie?" asked Mom. "Would you like some lunch?"

"I've had lunch, thanks, but a drink would be great," replied Hermie.

Mom turned to me. "Thebe, darling, be a sweetheart."

I put my package down, even though I was dying to see what was inside it. "What would you like?"

"Oh, just fix a tray, bring everything," said Mom,

her eyes still set on Hermie. "And use the best cups. The bone-china ones, if you can find them. Thebe's a dream child. A typical Virgo. She keeps this house running, don't you, love?" I was about to say yes, but Mom continued over me. "She's so organized and neat. The rest of us would forget to eat if she didn't do our weekly grocery shopping. Oh, yes, that child is a marvel. Now run along, darling, and fix a tray while your dad and I chat to Hermes here."

"Anything you don't like, Hermie?" I asked.

"Not really . . . oh, except honey. Don't bring me any honey. I . . . it has a strange effect on me . . ."

"Like an allergy?" asked Mom. "I'm that way with wheat."

Hermie nodded. "Sort of. All us planets are . . . um, allergic to honey."

"Think I read that in one of my books, Hermie," said Dad. "How does the allergy manifest?"

"Um . . . er . . . let's just say, best to be avoided."

"Sugar okay?" I asked.

Hermie nodded and smiled. "Sugar's fine."

I went into the kitchen, but I felt annoyed. According to the book, Hermie was my guardian, not theirs. The book said nothing about Zodiac *Parents*! But then, I couldn't stay mad at them for long. Of course they were as excited as I was. Astrology was their whole life, their passion, and to be meeting one of the planets in the flesh was like meeting their pinup or Hollywood hero. Plus, they were useless in the kitchen. Like, Mom might be great at business, but ask her to cook and she's a disaster. Once she flavored a simple jerk-chicken recipe with sugar instead of salt, and another time she put salt in the banana bread instead of sugar. Hopeless. Her mind is too busy wheeling and dealing. And Dad's no better. He can't even boil an egg. Pat used to help, but then she discovered boys, and working in the kitchen ruins her nails.

So it's up to me. I took over when I was ten. First thing I did was get a cleaner and a housekeeper to come in a couple of days a week and cook some meals for the freezer, and I do our grocery shopping on the Internet. I'm a whiz on the computer, and I enjoy getting everything organized. And one of my favorite things is rearranging the food cupboards so that everything can be found easily. It makes me feel happy when things are in the right places and done correctly—like I had a little ritual for preparing a meal tray: drinks first, food second, plates and silverware last. I poured a pitcher of pineapple-orange juice for our guest, and then I got the banana-and-coconut cake from the breadbox. I knew it was made with sugar and not honey because I'd cut the recipe out of a magazine and given it to the housekeeper myself. The finishing touch was to arrange plates, glasses, and napkins on the tray, and then I took it all in.

Mom, Dad, Hermie, and Pat were sitting on the sofa. Even Cosmo was in there, happily curled up on Hermie's knee! Pat didn't appear to be saying much. She was saying a lot with her body language, though. There was an article about speaking without words in last month's *Girl in the City* magazine. I could tell by the way Pat was sitting, with her skirt hitched up high and her body leaning forward, that she was saying, "Hello, handsome. Let's go for a ride on your motorcycle." Not that Mom or Dad noticed that their daughter was flirting so blatantly right in front of them. They only had eyes for Hermie. They were like two teenagers who had met their childhood crush and were sitting on the edge of the sofa, hanging onto his every word.

"Ah*em*." I coughed to let them know that I was back. Me. The Zodiac Girl. But no one noticed. As usual, I was the invisible member of our family. I put down the tray and went over to the desk where I'd left my package. As the others chatted away and wolfed down the juice and the cake, I unwrapped my present. Inside were two boxes, one smaller than the other. I opened that one first. Inside was a small jewelry box, and inside that was a silver chain with a tiny silver lady holding a sheaf of wheat. I'd seen necklaces like this before, as Mom had lots manufactured to sell on the website, but this one was exceptionally beautiful and delicate. I knew that the sheaf of wheat that the tiny lady was holding was supposed to symbolize wisdom. I glanced up to see if anyone had noticed that I was unwrapping my presents, but they were all still engrossed in their mutual-admiration club, so I opened the second box. Inside was the most divine cell phone. It was navy with a sprinkling of glitter, and at the top was a huge sapphire. It was stunning. I decided to butt into the conversation. "Hermie, thank you so much for my gorgeous presents."

"They're yours as a Zodiac Girl, Thebe. And the phone is so that you can get in touch with me and me with you."

At this point, I noticed Pat perk up even more. "Oh, really? Can I take a look, Thebe?"

Reluctantly, I handed over the phone.

"Oh my!" said Mom when she saw it. "It's lovely. We do a range of phones for each sign, but nothing as pretty as that. You must let me know your supplier. And it's interesting that it's blue with the sapphire. All the books seem to say something different about what the stone is for each sign. So much contradiction—like for Virgos, some books and websites say that navy is their color and others say green or shades of yellow. And some say sapphire is their birthstone and others say agate. What do you think, Hermie, sugar?"

And they were off again. I had wanted to ask

Hermie the same question that Mom had, but I had also wanted to say that I was glad my special phone had a sapphire on it, as that was my favorite stone and blue was my favorite color. But get a word in with this group? No way. My special day? The beginning of my special month?

It *so* wasn't meant to be like this.

Chapter Three

Surprise

"Are you a Zodiac Girl because your dad's a famous astrologer?" asked my best friend, Rachel, later that day as we sat on a bench and put on our skates at the local ice rink. I'd told her all about the visit and my Zodiac presents, and she was very impressed.

"No. It has nothing to do with Dad, or Mom for that matter," I said as I glanced out at the skaters flying by on the rink in front of us, "although you'd hardly know it by the way they took over the whole visit."

"So can I be a Zodiac Girl?"

"Maybe one day. There's a different one each month somewhere on the planet, and it depends on what's coming up in your horoscope. Hermie said that everyone reacts differently, and some girls make the most of their time, while others choose to ignore it altogether. He said they had one girl who stomped on her Zodiac phone and broke it. I can't imagine doing that—mine is so gorgeous. I'll show you at school tomorrow."

"Have you used it yet?"

"No. And I can only use it to get in touch with Hermie and the planet people, and he will use it to get in touch with me. It's like my hot line to them."

"What happens next?"

"I'm not sure, but it's going to be wonderful. Dad said he thinks that girls get chosen when they are at a crossroad or turning point in their lives. I'm not expecting any big changes in my life anytime soon, but who knows? Before he left, Hermie said that since Uranus features strongly in my chart, I should expect some kind of surprise. Uranus is the planet of the unexpected, and sometimes when he's around, things can happen out of nowhere, so really anything could happen."

"Wow. How exciting! I so wish I was a Zodiac Girl," said Rachel as she stood up and made her way onto the ice.

"So do I," I called after her, "but I promise I'll tell you all about it so you won't feel left out, and maybe you can meet Hermie one day."

"That would be so cool," said Rachel, and she pushed off the edge and skated perfectly into the center of the rink.

I felt bad about not being able to share being a Zodiac Girl with her—besides ice-skating, which is Rachel's thing, we shared everything. Clothes, jewelry, music, magazines. Her sign was Cancer, so I resolved to get her a Cancerian necklace from Mom's stock and also a cell-phone cover from a new range that Mom had designed. It wouldn't be the same as having the real thing, but it would be close enough so that Rachel wouldn't feel excluded.

"Come on," she called to me.

I took a deep breath. I'd been dreading this moment. I was totally horrible at ice-skating. I'd tried it twice when Rachel had first gotten into it, and I had fallen flat on my back both times. The only reason I was giving it another shot was that Dad's chosen celebrity for the month was Janet Johnson, an ice-skating champion, and she had invited my whole family to a party at the rink in four weeks' time. Since Mom and Dad and Pat are all confident skaters, I didn't want to be seen as the family failure, nor did I want to let down Dad.

I wobbled my way onto the rink and gingerly put my feet on the ice. Immediately I felt my lower half slide away but caught myself just in time and held onto the barrier surrounding the rink.

"Come on," Rachel called again.

"Mff," I mumbled. I was finding it hard to breath. There were too many people on the rink, and they were going so fast, whizzing past one another at a million miles an hour. *What if I fall?* I asked myself. *One of them might skate by and slice off my fingers with the blades of their skates.*

Rachel skated toward me. "You okay?" she asked.

I shook my head. "No. I can't do it. I'm sorry. I just can't."

She held out her arm to me. "Hold onto me—you'll be fine. I won't let you fall."

She was looking at me with such encouragement, but I couldn't do it. I couldn't let go. I felt like the ice. Frozen. "I can't, Rachel. I'm sorry."

"I was the same my first time," she said. "It gets easier; it really does. Just try a little bit—you can keep holding onto the side."

I still couldn't do it. My legs wouldn't move. I felt a huge knot in my stomach and was finding it hard to breathe.

"Next time," I wheezed. "I promise—I'll do it next time."

Rachel's such a great friend. She didn't push it. She just squeezed my arm. "You'll get there. You'll see. It just takes time."

I staggered off the ice and back to the safety of a nearby bench, where my breath slowed down to normal. I couldn't get the skates off fast enough. I sat and watched Rachel and the others for a while and felt miserable. *I'll have to come up with some excuse for getting out of the party*, I thought. *Pretend I have a cold or the flu or something, because at this rate I'm never going to be able to skate along with the others.*

When I got home later, I went downstairs to see what the others were doing. Dad was taking a nap on a sofa in the study with his headphones on and Mom was at the other end of the sofa, doing work on her laptop. The French windows were open, and a warm breeze wafted in from the yard.

"Hey, hon," she said, without looking up from the screen, when I walked in. "How was the skating?"

"Fine," I lied. "Um . . . what you doing?"

"I'm preparing a press release to say that the planets are here in human form and that one of them visited us here today."

"No! *No*, Mom! You can't do that."

"Why ever not, baby? This is the opportunity of a lifetime. Just think of the business it's going to bring us."

My head filled with a series of horrible images. People teasing me at school, for a start. It was one thing telling Rachel about being a Zodiac Girl, but if it got around school, I'd be a laughingstock. My family stood out as unusual as it was, and I had wised up pretty fast to the fact that not everyone believed in astrology and that some people even thought it was complete nonsense and that wackos believed in it. If it got out that my family thought that the planets were here in human form, people would think we really were bananas. No. It couldn't happen. Plus the fact that Hermie and the rest of the planets must feel free to come and go at our house. The last thing they'd want was to be hounded by paparazzi.

"Dad. *Dad*. Wake up," I said, tugging on Dad's toes until he opened his eyes. He took off his headphones and sat up.

"What's going on?" he asked.

"It's Mom. You have to stop her. She wants to tell the press that the planets are here in human form. I . . . I don't think we should tell anyone."

Dad shook his head. "Estella, Thebe's right about this one. Let it go."

"But baby . . ."

"No. We don't want the planet people to feel uncomfortable coming here now, do we? We want this to be a haven for them, so we're going to keep it quiet. In the family. The press would treat them like freaks. It's a no-no."

Mom stuck out her bottom lip like a five-year-old.

"Come on now—you know we're right," said Dad.

Mom folded her arms across her stomach and pouted even more. She didn't like not getting her own way.

"I don't often put my foot down, Estella, but I'm going to about this. We are hosts for the honored guests and that's it. Just having them here will be wonderful, and think what we can learn. It can help business that way and maybe even give us more ideas for merchandising, but *no* press and that's final."

I glanced over at Mom to see how she was going to react. She'd gone all coy and girlie and was looking up at Dad, batting her eyelashes. "Oh, Benjie," she said. "I *love* it when you're forceful."

Oh for God's sake, I thought. *I hope they don't start kissing in front of me. That would be so disgusting.*

"You hear me, Estella—I mean it," said Dad, clearly relishing the effect he was having on Mom.

"Oh, I hear you, Mr. Battye, you big lug you," she said, and then she clapped her hands. "We'll have lots of tea parties for them. Dinner parties. Thebe, darling, invite them all over as soon as you can. We can get Nikkya to cater so that they can sample authentic Caribbean food. What do you think? Thebe, be sure to find out if any of them are vegetarians or have any special dietary needs besides that honey thing." (Auntie Nikkya has her own restaurant that serves delicious Caribbean food, the kind Mom used to attempt to make before she became Businesswoman of the Year. We usually ordered dinner from Auntie at least once a week.)

Dad and I looked at each other and smiled. Mom was off again, but at least it was in a safe direction this time.

"But Mom, I don't know how it works exactly. I

don't even know if I'll get to meet all ten planets. Hermie said most Zodiac Girls get to meet the ones who are prevalent in their charts."

"So look at your chart, child. What are you waiting for?"

"I'm waiting for Hermie, my guardian, to contact me to tell me what's next. He said something about Uranus, but that was all . . . But you're right—we should be able to figure out some of what's coming up for me by ourselves."

Dad got my chart down from where he'd stuck it onto the wall near his desk, and the three of us bent over it.

"Hmm, looks like some conflict coming up, munchkin," said Dad. "Uranus, yes, we know about that—a surprise on its way—although that could have been the fact that you got to be a Zodiac Girl. That's a surprise. What else? Hmm, the Moon, yes, emotions stirred up, but the Moon always does that."

"Yes, but nothing major?" I asked.

"Speaking of conflict," said Mom as she suddenly lost interest in my chart and picked up another one that was lying in Dad's in box. "You seen this?"

Dad looked over. "Your sister's chart."

Mom nodded. "Now that's what I call conflict. Mars, Venus, and the Moon squared up against one another. I think she's finally going to split with Norrece."

THEBE'S CHART

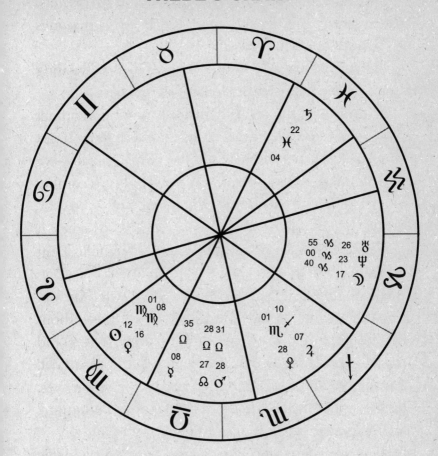

SYMBOLS OF THE PLANETS AND SIGNS

☉	☽	☿	♀	♈	♉	♊	♋	♌
SUN	MOON	MERCURY	VENUS	ARIES	TAURUS	GEMINI	CANCER	LEO

♂	♃	♄	♅	♍	♎	♏	✗
MARS	JUPITER	SATURN	URANUS	VIRGO	LIBRA	SCORPIO	SAGITTARIUS

♆	♇	♑	♒	♓
NEPTUNE	PLUTO	CAPRICORN	AQUARIUS	PISCES

Dad nodded. "I saw his chart, too. It does indicate a rift of sorts."

"Understatement," said Mom.

"Um, Earth to Mom and Dad. Zodiac Girl here," I said. "I thought we were looking at *my* chart."

Mom waved the air as if dismissing me. "No, hon, you got it right. Hermie will be in touch. How about you go check the kitchen supplies while your father and I discuss my sister? If we're going to be entertaining, we need to have plenty of food and drinks."

I sighed. For a brief second there, I thought I was actually going to be the center of attention. But no. It was a shame that Auntie Mattie and Uncle Norrece might break up, though. I was sad to hear that. I liked them both, but it was true—they did argue a lot. They were both Leos. Leo is the sign of the lion, and anyone born in that month likes to be the king of the jungle, which is hard if there are two of you battling for the place. Leos can also roar like lions, and boy, it was noisy when those two came over and weren't getting along. However, like all Leos, they also had big hearts and were very generous, and that made up for all the growling. They had a daughter, Yasmin, and as much as Uncle Norrece and Auntie Mattie could be charm personified, Yasmin was misery on a stick. She was 15 and bossy and sullen, unless you were a boy, in which case she suddenly became Little Miss Sunshine. She was a Gemini, and they can be very flirty. She called me Miss Prissy Pants just because she came across me color-coding my wardrobe one rainy afternoon when they were visiting. When I tried to explain that I was doing it so I could find things easily, she said, "Oh, get a life, loser." I hate her. With some luck, if Auntie Mattie and Uncle Norrece do split up, Yasmin will get sent somewhere far away and I'll never have to see her ever again. Somewhere like Australia. Or the Moon.

"Hey, Dad, how do you think the Sun is manifested down here?" I asked. "I forgot to ask Hermie who they all were here and what they did."

"Oh, we asked him while you were in the kitchen," said Mom.

"And you didn't tell me! Mo-*om*. I am the Zodiac Girl, you know, not you."

Mom chuckled and tickled me under the chin. "Ooh, you's so sweet when you's angry. Isn't she cute when she's angry, Benjamin?"

Dad began tickling me, too, and soon I was splayed across one of the sofas laughing and gasping for breath. I am the most ticklish person in the world. "Just *tell* me what the other planets are, Dad," I gasped as they let me go.

"Um, let me remember. Okay. Hermie—"

"Motorcycle messenger," I said.

"Correct," said Dad. "Venus. Now tell me about Venus, Thebe."

I sighed. This is how I got to know everything I did about astrology—Dad turned every simple question into an opportunity to teach me a lesson. "Venus rules Taureans and Librans and is the planet of love and beauty," I replied.

"Correct. And she runs a beauty salon in Osbury, and in the evenings she teaches classes about how to discover your inner goddess."

"Cool," I said and got a piece of paper from Dad's desk to write down the names of the planet people.

"She should run a dating agency," said Mom. "If we meet her, I'm going to tell her. It would be perfect for her."

"Um, Mom, I think they are here to tell us—that is me—what to do, not the other way around."

"Says who? There are no rules. Did Hermie give you a set of rules?"

"No, Mom. Do Mars next, Dad. And before you ask, Mars is the ruler of Aries, the god of war."

"Ex-Marine, teaches karate and self-defense classes," said Dad.

"Excellent, obvious," I said as I added Mars to my list.

"See if you can guess the next one, hon," said

Mom. "Let's do . . . Jupiter."

"Planet of merriment and expansion that rules Sagittarius," I said. "Hmm. Clown?"

Mom shook her head.

"Caterer?"

"Close," said Dad. "He runs a deli in Osbury. Venus is called Nessa down here, by the way, and he's called Joe."

"Okay. Let's guess for Uranus," I said. "Rules Aquarius, planet of the unexpected and magic. Hmm, magician?"

"Again, not a bad guess, Thebe," said Dad. "He runs a magic shop and an Internet café. His name is Uri and he's also in Osbury. I just knew they'd all be around here somewhere."

"So who's left?" asked Mom.

"The Moon, Sun, Neptune, Saturn, and Pluto," I said.

"Saturn, the taskmaster. He's here as a Dr. Cronus, a headmaster at a private school," said Dad.

"Perfect," I said as I wrote that down.

"Pluto, the planet of transformation," said Dad. "He's an interior designer. Neptune, the lord of dreams and the king of the sea, he runs a fish-and-chips restaurant and I do believe owns a couple of boats and takes tourists out for day trips."

Our discussion was cut short by the sound of the

phone ringing. Mom picked up, and I could tell by the expression on her face that it was bad news. After a few minutes, she put down the phone and turned to face us.

"As I thought. Mattie and Norrece are going their separate ways. At least for a while."

"What are they going to do?" asked Dad.

"Take a little time out to think things over. She's going to stay with relatives in Jamaica. He's going to an island in Greece to chill out and think about what he wants."

"Is Yasmin going with her mother?" asked Dad.

Mom shook her head. "You know you can't just leave school in the middle of the semester. Plus, they don't want her falling behind. They've asked if she can stay here. It's just for a month."

"A month!" I blurted. *An hour with Yasmin here would be enough to drive me insane*, I thought.

"Uh-huh. A month. So Thebe, hon, you've got the biggest room, so she's going to have to share with you."

"*Me?* But what about the spare room?"

Mom and Dad both cracked up. The "spare" room, which had been decorated as the Saturn room, was anything but spare at the moment. It was stuffed as high as the ceiling with merchandise samples for Mom's business, plus anything else that we couldn't find space for—bikes, old toys, Rollerblades, books, old clothes, and shoes in black trash bags. It was like a thrift store in there, and you could hardly get the door open—it was so full. Cleaning it up and throwing out stuff was on my "to do" list.

"We could empty it," I said. "We've been meaning to make it into a real spare room for months."

"We could," Mom agreed, "but she's coming tomorrow. We'd never get it done by then. Besides, where would we put all that stuff? The garage is piled high, too."

"Why can't she share with Pat?"

"Because Pat's studying for her SATs and the loft room doesn't have space for another bed. Plus, Yasmin needs space and quiet to study and you have a spare bed in your room."

It was true. I had a bed in there for Rachel's sleepovers. I was just scanning my mind for any other alternative (like a tent in the yard!) when my Zodiac phone beeped that I had a text message.

"Ooh, it's the Zodiaphone," said Mom. "Let's see. Let's see."

I quickly took a look in the hope that it might be some *good* news.

"Surprises aren't always what you think. Love, Uri," said the text message.

Dad cracked up laughing. "Can't argue with that, can you, munchkin?" he asked. "And Uranus is also the planet of rebellion as well as the planet of surprises. Now, are you going to get all rebellious on us?"

Mom laughed, too, but I couldn't join in with them. *No. No. NO. NOOOOOOOOOOOOOOO*, I thought. *Yasmin coming to stay can't be my surprise. It is my Zodiac month. It's supposed to be the best month ever. This has to be some kind of mistake.*

Chapter Four

Roommate from Hades

<u>Thebe's list of things to do</u>

1) Clean room and get Mrs. W. to make up
    bed for Yasmin.
2) Put flowers and fruit next to her bed
    to make Yasmin feel welcome.
3) Call Hermie to synchronize diaries for
    my Zodiac month.
4) Do homework.
5) Practice ice-skating.

"And that scraggly thing can think again about coming in here," said Yasmin as she picked up Cosmo and shoved him out into the hall. He looked up at me accusingly, and I tried to communicate by telepathy that I was sorry. It wasn't my decision. He wasn't appeased. He looked how I felt. Disgruntled. He padded off down the corridor toward Mom and Dad's room with his tail down. It wasn't fair. Yasmin had only been in my room ten minutes and already she was taking over.

"His *name* is Cosmo and he always sleeps in here," I protested. "It's *his* home."

"But . . . uh, I'm allergic, a . . . a . . . chooo," said Yasmin in a totally fake stuffed-up voice. I knew stuffed up when I heard it because I genuinely suffered from allergies. Pollen. Wheat. Dust. All sorts of things brought it on (although luckily cats isn't one of them), and Yasmin was clearly putting on the sniffles to get her own way. She just didn't like cats.

The next thing she did was go to the closet and pull out five hangers with my clothes on them. She laid them over the back of my desk chair.

"But . . . but I already made some space for you," I said as I indicated the free area to the right of my clothes.

"I'm *fifteen*. I have more clothes than you. We older girls need more than little girls," she said as she went back to her bed, opened her suitcase, and turned it upside down so that stuff spilled out onto the mattress and then onto the floor. She put away a few things, and then she began to pile books from the bookshelf next to my desk onto the floor.

"What are you doing?" I asked as I sat on my bed and watched her.

"Making a line," she replied as she laid out the books like the foundation of a brick wall. When she'd made a line from one side of the room to the other, she stood up and indicated the area on one side of the line. "Now this is my side, okay?" Then she indicated the side with my bed. "And that's yours, okay? No crossing over." She then turned her back on me, threw herself onto her bed, and put on her iPod headphones. She was clearly no happier about the change in her living arrangements than I was, although earlier in the day I had resolved to make the most of the situation and welcome her to the house. I'd even gone out and bought some flowers with my allowance money for the table beside her bed and put a bowl of oranges there, too.

I don't know why I bothered, I thought as I made myself bite back what was on the tip of my tongue. I was dying to say that actually it was *my* room and she was *my* guest, but Mom had given me a lecture about how Yasmin's parents breaking up must be hard on her and we must all be kind and treat her with kid gloves. I knew what kind of gloves I'd like to treat her with and they weren't kid gloves—they were boxing gloves. I'd like to sock her right on her pretty lip-glossed kisser. Sometimes I even surprise myself with how violent my thoughts can be.

Suddenly, Yasmin took off her headphones and turned toward me. "And what is this room anyway?" she asked as she looked around at the décor. "It's not normal."

My bedroom was the Venus room in the house, and Mom and I had decided that seeing as Venus is the goddess of love and beauty, it should be the most beautiful room in the house. Venus is the second-closest planet to the Sun, and after the Moon it is the brightest object in the night sky. Venus is also known as the morning or evening star (even though it's a planet!), so when we started decorating, I thought it was only natural to go with a star theme. We'd painted the walls white, and then all around the top I'd stenciled in stars. The lamp in the center of the room was a silver star and the bedspreads were white, but the pillowcases were silver. It looked clean and neat and I loved it.

On the wall between the two beds was a mural that Auntie Francelle had done. (She's the artist in the family and had done a number of the paintings around the house, including some in Dad's study—and of course she works as part of Battye Enterprises and designs cards and posters for Mom.) My mural depicted the goddess Venus with long hair curved around her body. It was actually a copy of a painting I'd seen in a book once by the Italian artist Sandro Botticelli. It was called *The Birth of Venus*. I couldn't wait to show it to the real Venus when she showed up, which, according to a text message I'd gotten last night from Hermie, was probably going to be in the next couple of days. "Venus and the Moon," he'd said. He also indicated that there was going to be a difficult aspect, but that was to be expected with old grumpy goat Yasmin showing up. I really hoped that the Moon and Venus would come over in person like Hermie had. That would be so cool.

"That is nasty," said Yasmin, pointing to the mural. She got up from the bed and picked up a roll of paper from her things on the floor. "In fact, seeing as some of the wall where it's painted comes over on my side of the room, I'm going to put this over it." She unrolled a poster of a huge red pair of lips with a tongue sticking out; underneath it, it said, "People Suck." She taped it to the wall.

"Nooo," I said. "That looks awful there. Please. Be reasonable. And it covers up Auntie Francelle's work."

Yasmin shrugged. "So bite me," she said. "Your mom said we had to share and that we had to be nice to each other, right? I'm going through a life trauma, so you've got to go easy on me. Right?"

She had me. "Right, but . . . can't you see it just doesn't go with the rest of the room?"

Yasmin laughed. "Since when have you become Queen of Interior Design? Your mom said to make myself at home and that's what I'm doing. Would you like me to go and tell her that you're making me feel unwelcome?"

"No, of course not." *Maybe I am being a tad unwelcoming*, I thought, and I resolved to be kinder. I knew I wouldn't like it if my mom and dad were splitting up and I had to uproot and go stay with another family. "I'm sorry. Of course you can put up your poster."

Yasmin smiled. I think she knew that I didn't have a leg to stand on. And then I remembered. I wasn't alone in this. I was a Zodiac Girl. The planets were here to help me for my special month. Maybe there was a message of support or some advice from Hermie as to how to deal with my new roommate. I went to my desk (which was only just over my side) and got my Zodiac phone from the drawer.

Yasmin immediately perked up. "What's that?"

"Um. A phone."

"I can see that. Where did you get it?"

"Oh. Don't know. It was a present. It's for my birth sign."

Yasmin nodded. "It's cool. Could your mom get me one like that?"

"Doubt it," I said, "and anyhow, you're not a Virgo like me, so one in this color and with this stone on it wouldn't be right for your sign. You're a Gemini and—"

"Like I care one bit about that garbage," Yasmin interrupted, "but it is a cool phone. Let me take a look."

I passed the phone to her, and she pressed a few buttons and turned it over. "Doesn't seem to be working."

"It was working earlier," I said, and I prayed that she hadn't pressed something wrong and broken it.

She tossed it back to me. "Not much use if it doesn't work," she said, and then she pulled out some small speakers from her pile on the floor. She plugged her iPod into them, and the room filled with really LOUD, head-banging music. She sat back down on her bed and gave me a smug smile. "Cool tunes, huh?"

I winced. "Not the word I'd have used to describe it," I said, and I began to clean up my side of the room in the hope that she might see my good example and learn from it.

Yasmin laughed. "Jeez, Thebe, anyone ever told you that you're like an old lady?" she asked as she reached out, took an orange, and lay back against the pillows and began to peel it. When she was finished, she threw the peel onto the floor and began to pop segments of the orange into her mouth.

I stepped over the line of books, picked up the peel, and put it into the wastebasket under my desk. In response, Yasmin turned up her music even higher.

I looked at my phone and pressed the button that Hermie had told me to use in order to reach him. It seemed to be working again. I texted my message.

"Please help. Urgent. Cousin came to stay. Not friendly. What should I do?"

A message beeped right back.

"Mercury has gone retrograde. Hermie is unavailable at the moment. Call back later."

Oh no, I thought. I knew what Mercury going retrograde meant. It happened regularly throughout the year, usually three times, but I so hoped that it didn't mean that I wasn't going to be able to get ahold of my guardian on the very month that I was a Zodiac Girl. That would be so unfair. Like winning the lottery but finding out that you'd lost the winning ticket. I went downstairs to see if Dad might be able to shed any light on the situation.

"Dad, Mercury's gone retrograde," I said as I burst into his study to find that there was someone with him. "Oh, sorry, I didn't realize that you had company." Sitting across from Dad was a man with a big silver-gray beard and a smiling, weather-beaten face. He was wearing a sea captain's hat and a classy navy blazer. Dad and he were drinking and chatting.

"Ah! Is this the Zodiac Girl?" asked the man.

I nodded and looked to Dad for an explanation. Dad grinned. "Thebe, meet Captain John Dory."

"Oh, hi, Captain Jo—"

"Also known as Neptune!" said Dad.

"No kidding? Wow! Hi. I . . ." I went over to the wall and glanced at my chart. There didn't seem to be any strong link to Neptune that I could see, and Hermie hadn't mentioned anything about a visit from Captain John in his earlier messages.

"So how's your time as a Zodiac Girl going, Thebe?"

asked the captain.

"Oh. Fine, I guess. Early days. Um . . . but I wasn't expecting you. It's not in my chart at the moment. I was expecting Venus and the Moon. What are you doing here?"

Dad frowned at me as if I'd said something wrong. "Now then, Thebe, all of the planets are welcome in this house. It doesn't have to be in your chart for them to come by. Indeed no. Captain John, you can come by anytime."

Captain John raised his glass. "That's good of you, Benjamin," he said, and then he turned to me. "And actually, all us planets affect your chart, Thebe; you should know that. Yes, some are more prevalent at certain times, but even those in the background have an influence. Now, as far as I can remember, you have your Neptune in Capricorn. Know what that means?"

"Um . . . Neptune has to do with dreams and ideals, doesn't it? I mean you?"

The captain nodded. "And in your case, you have very high expectations. High ideals."

I nodded. "Mom always taught us to have goals."

The captain nodded again. "But make them reasonable ones, Thebe. You might find that you have to lower your expectations now and then."

I nodded back, but I was unsure exactly what he meant. Did it have to do with my being a Zodiac Girl?

No way was I going to lower my expectations for that. Why should I? Hermie had said that some Zodiac Girls let the opportunity pass by, and I certainly didn't want that to happen. I wanted to be a girl who made every single moment of it count—which reminded me of Hermie. "So Dad, Mercury has gone retrograde. What will that mean for me as a Zodiac Girl? Especially since he's my guardian."

"It will be for around three weeks," said Captain John. "Mercury retrograde usually means miscommunication, misunderstandings of some sort, computers crashing, phones not working, things going missing."

"In my case, it seems to be Hermie himself," I said.

Dad and the captain nodded.

"Best not to make any important decisions at the moment," said the captain. "Mercury is all about mental clarity, so when he's retrograde, your judgment can be clouded. Still, it's only for three weeks."

"Three weeks! But it can't be. I mean, surely that can't be right. I mean . . . will he be around at all?" I blustered.

Captain John shrugged. "Maybe, maybe not. You can never be certain of anything when Mercury goes retrograde."

I glanced over at the captain. I really wanted some time alone with Dad to discuss my chart and make plans for how best to make use of my time. "Um . . . Dad . . ."

Dad took a sip of his beer. "Just go with the flow, baby," he said, and then he turned his attention back to his visitor. "Just go with the flow and all will be well, and in the meantime the captain here and I have a lot of things to talk about, so be a dear and run along, okay?"

"Good advice—to go with the flow," said Captain John. "And Thebe, believe in your dreams."

Pff, I thought as I left the room. *Go with the flow? Run along. Ha! What did Dad know? I can't "flow" back up to my room, which is what I'd really like to do, because it's too noisy in there with my roommate from Hades.* I kicked the wall with frustration.

"Ow!" I cried as my toe throbbed with pain. I went up the stairs to the second floor and listened at my bedroom door. Yasmin was still playing music at full volume in there. I went up the next flight of stairs. Maybe I could hang out in Pat's room and read a book. Her door was locked. I knocked. "Pat, you in there?"

"Go away," came her voice from inside.

"Please," I said. "I won't get in your way."

"You've got your own room."

"Nope. Yasmin's taken over."

"Then go see what Mom's doing. I'm busy."

I sighed and set off back down the stairs and along to Mom and Dad's bedroom, which was the Aquarius room. When I opened the door, I saw that the silver velvet curtains were closed, with the only light coming from a lavender scented candle on Mom's dressing table, and some gentle New Age music was playing. It felt cool and peaceful in there. The walls were painted electric blue. Mom and I had done some stenciling along the top of the walls similar to my room, only instead of stars we'd done a series of silver streaks of lightning. These symbolized the energy of Uranus, the ruling planet of Aquarius, which was often said to come out of the blue. Mom was lying on the bed in her bathrobe and looked like something out of a horror movie. Her hair was scraped back in a headband, her face was plastered white, and she had cucumber slices over both eyes.

"Mom . . ." I whispered.

"Erf. Oo ee it?"

"Thebe."

"Erf 'ace 'ask," she said through her closed mouth. I understood. Face mask. She didn't like to say much when she had one on in case it cracked.

"Can I stay in here for a while?"

"Uh-uh," she said as she shook her head from side to side. Mom took her chill-out time *very* seriously. I got the message.

Not wanted upstairs. Not wanted downstairs. Not wanted in my own room, I thought as I trooped down to the kitchen. Outside it was pouring rain, so the yard wasn't an option. *Go with the flow, Dad had said. What stupid flow? I'm the only one who really understands what it takes to keep things flowing. I really am,* I thought as I stomped off into the laundry room at the back of the kitchen to sort the dirty clothes into light- and dark-colored piles, ready for Mrs. Watson, who was coming in tomorrow morning. *If this family went with the flow, there would be no food, no dinner, no clean clothes. The house would be a total mess if it wasn't for me getting things organized!*

Above the dryer was one of Mom's charts listing all of the signs of the zodiac and their symbols.

Aries: the ram
Taurus: the bull
Gemini: the twins
Cancer: the crab
Leo: the lion
Virgo: the virgin
Libra: the scales
Scorpio: the scorpion
Sagittarius: the archer
Capricorn: the goat
Aquarius: the water carrier
Pisces: two fish

It was a nice poster, with illustrations of each symbol drawn by Auntie Francelle, but I stuck out my tongue at it. I felt angry. Being part of a zodiac family, living in a zodiac house, and being a Zodiac Girl wasn't any fun at all!

From one of Dad's books on astrology:

The word *retrograde* applies, in astrology, to the *apparent* backward motion through the zodiac of a planet. All of the planets, except the Sun and Moon, have these retrograde periods, but Mercury is most famous for them, probably because Mercury represents communication.

This includes writing, speaking, shopping, and signing contracts. While Mercury is retrograde, don't give that party, be extra careful what you say and what you interpret when chatting with or writing to friends, and expect mail to take longer than usual and computers to crash, so make sure you back up anything important.

Good things to do when Mercury is retrograde are: chill out, meditate, edit that book/poem/song/essay you've been writing, clean the house, talk to your pet, listen to music, paint, catch up on sleep!

Chapter Five

Queen of Sheba

"You're telling me that nothing's happened?" asked Rachel the next day at school when I told her about my first weekend as a Zodiac Girl. She looked as disappointed as I felt. "I thought you'd have been having a fantastic time, with all sorts of magical things happening."

"Maybe that's how it is for some Zodiac Girls, but not for this one, Thebe Battye. I must be so uninspiring and ordinary that the planets can't even be bothered to think of anything exciting for me to do, and even my guardian's run off—he's so bored."

"You're not boring, Thebe," said Rachel, and she squeezed my arm. "I think you're the most interesting girl in the whole school." Rachel has been my best friend since elementary school. Dad used to call us Ebony and Ivory after a song written by Paul McCartney, who was Dad's favorite Beatle. It has something to do with piano keys, I think. The lyrics are "Ebony and ivory play together in perfect harmony," or something like that. We're total opposites in looks—

Rachel is tall with long blond hair and creamy white skin and I'm small and dark with coffee-colored skin.

I smiled. It was nice of her to say that, but what I knew she really meant was that my *family* was interesting and where I *lived* was interesting. I was only interesting because I basked in their reflections. It was only a matter of time before she realized that I was the black sheep of the family. I was the dull one.

After school, I went to the ice rink to try to get some practice in without anyone I knew witnessing my shame, but for all my best intentions, I still couldn't let go of the edge or stand up on my own. I made my way home afterward feeling like a failure and hoped that I could have my room to myself for half an hour before Yasmin got back from school. I was hoping to clean up and get the room organized after the mess she'd made everywhere—seeing everything neat and clean always made me feel better again.

I let myself in and was about to go make a peanut butter and jelly sandwich (with rye bread, as I'm allergic to wheat) when I heard the sound of laughter and chattering coming from Dad's study. I knocked on the door in case he had a client with him, but there was no response and the laughter continued. In the end, my curiosity got the better of me, so I opened the door and stuck in my head. Captain John Dory was back, but this time he had someone else with him. He was much older looking than the captain, had a long white beard, wore small glasses, and was dressed in an old-fashioned-looking tweed suit. He was engrossed in one of Dad's old books. And then it dawned on me. *If Captain John Dory is here, maybe the other man is one of the planet people, too.*

"Ah, here she is," said Dad when he spotted me. "Come on in, Thebe. We've got guests!"

Mom bustled in from behind me with a tray of drinks and a big smile. "Sorry, guys, it's cranberry and apple juice since we don't have any nectar of the gods today. Maybe next time."

The guests cracked up laughing, like Mom had said the funniest thing ever.

"Thebe, come in. Meet everyone," said Dad. "Captain John Dory, you know. And this is Dr. Cronus, AKA Saturn." The man in glasses nodded in my direction.

I did my best to smile in a friendly manner, but I wasn't sure what to say or how to act. How to greet planets that manifest in human form hadn't been covered at school. I felt like I was going to faint or my brain was going to short-circuit. And then I remembered what a mess the Saturn room was upstairs. I so hoped that Mom and Dad hadn't shown him up there or else he might have gotten upset.

"Um, have you had a grand tour of the house?" I asked, trying to sound casual.

"First floor only," Dr. Cronus replied. "My old bones can't do the stairs like I used to."

Thank heavens for that, I thought. *Still, it's strange that he's in here with Neptune and Dad and doesn't seem that bothered about talking to me. I remember that Hermie mentioned something about Saturn in my chart before he took off, but I don't remember him saying anything about Neptune, so what's he doing here? I know. Maybe he's come over to make up for Hermie disappearing and he's come with Dr. Cronus to introduce themselves and congratulate me on being a Zodiac Girl.*

However, it wasn't just the fact that they were there that was making me feel unsettled—it was the atmosphere in the room. It was like there had been a surge in electricity or someone had turned on the heat to full blast. The room felt like it was bubbling with an energy that was so alive that it seemed like it might break down the walls.

"Um . . . no Hermie?" I asked.

"Retrograde," chorused everyone, and then they all laughed again.

"Now, Thebe, I'm sure you have homework to do," said Dad.

"Yes. It's very important to do your homework," said Dr. Cronus, and he gave me a stern look over his glasses. I remembered that Mom had said that Saturn was the taskmaster of the zodiac, the one who taught important lessons, and that his human guise was that of a school's headmaster. I could see that he'd be a very strict one and was glad that he wasn't the principal at my school.

"I always do my homework," I told him. I did. I was an A student and was never late with work. It was important to me to always do the best I could, both at home and at school.

Dr. Cronus observed me for a few moments, which made me feel more uncomfortable than ever, and then he turned away as if he'd lost interest. *Oh God, he can see how boring I am*, I thought as I tugged on Mom's arm. At first she took no notice, as she seemed intent on chatting with the guests, but eventually she gave in and came out with me to the hallway.

"What is it, Thebe?" she asked.

"Mom, I'm not sure that both Neptune and Saturn should be here today. Hermie told me that Zodiac Girls only get to meet those who are prevalent in their chart in their special month. I think Saturn is supposed to be here, but the only others who should be are the Moon and Venus."

Mom patted my head. "Oh chill, Thebe, honey. These guys aren't here to see *you*. They're here to see *us*. Your father invited them over to look at his library and to . . . well, to talk stars. And they seem as eager as we are. Joe Jupiter stopped by this afternoon, too, while you were at school. They are so interested to find out how astrology is perceived in this day and age, and they're dying to see all my merchandise. Now, don't you worry your pretty little head about them. You run along upstairs."

There it was again—*run along*. Mom must have seen my face fall because she pointed upstairs. "You have your own guests. Up there."

"Me? Who?"

"What were you just telling me about the Moon and Venus? You were right and they *are* here. Pat took them up, and I think Yasmin's home, too."

Oh lollipops, the Moon and Venus alone with Pat and Yasmin, yiiiiiiiiiiiiiikes, I thought as I took the stairs two at a time and prayed that my sister and my cousin hadn't put off my planet guides for good. I burst into my room to see the kind of scene that you'd find in any girl's bedroom. A woman with long blond hair had her back to me and was braiding Yasmin's hair, while Pat was relaxing on my bed. By the way she was holding up her hands, she had clearly had her nails done recently.

"Hey, Thebe," said Pat. "This is Nessa. She's come from a beauty salon in—where was it, Nessa?"

"Osbury, dahlin'," said the woman in a Southern accent as she turned to me and smiled. She was the most beautiful woman I had ever seen in my life. She had a perfect heart-shaped face, white blond hair, sky blue eyes, and a smile that lit up the room. I was thrown for a moment. Was she Venus? Could she be? She was certainly stunning enough, but would a goddess-type planet person wear tight white jeans, even if they did have little diamante sequins running along the seams? And her T-shirt looked totally up-to-date—there was nothing ancient about it at all. Somehow, though, I'd imagined that Venus would wear goddess-type clothes, but the woman in our room was pure rock star's wife trendy. "Hi there, Thebe."

"Are . . . you . . . you . . . Venus?" I whispered.

Yasmin cracked up. "Venus schmemus. D'oh! Time for your medication, Thebe."

Pat rolled her eyes up to the ceiling. "Take no notice, Ness," she said. "My little sister—in fact, my whole family—is crazy about the stars."

"Is that right?" said Nessa, and she kept her eyes on me and then winked. I was certain who she was then. And she knew that I knew. It didn't matter what my stupid sister said. Or my cousin. Nessa *was* Venus.

"What do you . . . ? That is . . . do you like the room?" I asked.

Nessa looked around in appreciation. "Just love it," she said, and her glance stopped on the mural that had been partially covered by Yasmin's horrible poster. "Shame you can't see that fantastic paintin', though. Based on a Botticelli, isn't it?"

I nodded. "*The Birth of Venus*."

"That's what I thought," said Yasmin, getting up and taking down the poster immediately. "Such a shame not to see all of it."

I couldn't believe how she was sucking up. I *so* wanted Pat and Yasmin to get out so that I could have a real talk with Nessa. There were so many things I wanted to ask her, but they seemed intent on staying. And stay they did. They talked about hair and makeup and skin care, even how to wax your legs, and Nessa didn't seem to mind at all. She finished Yasmin's hair. She painted Pat's toenails. She showed both of them how to make the most of their lips. She offered to show me how to do my makeup, too, but I wasn't bothered about that. I had much more important things to ask her about. I felt myself getting angry again. *What's the point of being a Zodiac Girl*, I thought, *if you have to share it with your stupid relatives?*

"Um . . . is there anyone else with you?" I asked, when I suddenly realized that Mom had said something about the Moon having arrived with Venus.

"Oh yeah," said Nessa, and she looked around as if expecting someone else to appear out of nowhere. "Selene was with us when your mom gave us the tour of the house when we first got here. Where'd she go?"

Pat and Yasmin shrugged.

"She asked where the bathroom was," said Pat. "Maybe she's in there."

I set off to look. Maybe the Moon lady would be more interested in *me*. But then again, with my luck, she probably wouldn't.

I found her sitting halfway up the stairs to Pat's room. She had the look of a mermaid about her, although without the tail, as I could clearly see two feet with sparkly nails in silver sandals poking out from underneath her ankle-length skirt. Her clothes were made from a luminous pale gray-green silky material, the color of fish's scales, and she had long silver-white hair that fell over her face. She was leaning over with her head in her hands, and she didn't look happy at all.

"Um . . . are you all right?" I asked as I approached as quietly as I could.

She looked up, and I saw that her eyes were the color of the sea—aquamarine—and the irises were outlined with deep jade green. On her forehead she had a silver dot. She was very striking, but in a different way to Nessa. Nessa was in-your-face obvious gorgeous, whereas this woman was gentler looking, with a quieter beauty.

"Oh!" she said.

I sat beside her. "I . . um . . . I'm Thebe."

"Oh," she said again. "Zodiac Girl?"

I nodded. "Are you Selene?"

She nodded. "Selene Luna."

"The Moon," I said, and then I couldn't think of anything else to say, so we both sat in silence for a few minutes. "Um . . . is there something the matter?"

Selene sniffed, and it was then that I realized that she'd been crying. I put my hand on her arm. "Oh, don't cry—it can't be all that bad. What is it? You can tell me. I'm a good listener."

Selene sniffed again and pointed upstairs. "Your mom gave us the tour when we arrived. Beautiful room after beautiful room. The house is . . . lovely."

"I know. Mom's very proud of the décor. Our house was even featured in *Heavenly Homes* magazine one month. Did you see my room?"

Selene nodded. "Yes . . ." *Sniff, sniff.* "It's really nice. It's . . . all . . . lovely . . ." *Sob, sob.*

"So what is it? Should I get Mom? She really wanted you all to feel at home here." And then I realized. How could I have been so insensitive? There was no Moon room. It had been painted over. "Oh peanuts! No Moon room. Oh, Selene, I am so sorry. There used to be. It was up there and it was lovely, it really was, magical, and then . . . my sister Pat . . ."

"I know. Painted over it. Ten planets and I'm the only one who got covered over."

"Not exactly. The Saturn room is stuffed to the ceiling with Mom's merchandise and anything that won't fit in any other room."

"Yes, but underneath all that it's still the Saturn room, isn't it? But mine's been removed. Painted over. It happens all the time, you know. Like I'm invisible

64

sometimes. People don't realize how hard it is for me. I try my best, you know, I really do. I try to shine, I put out as much light as I can, but it's never enough. It's because I don't have my *own* light, did you know that? I shine by the sunlight reflected from my surface. Without the Sun, I'm nothing but a cold, rocky place . . . I am sooooo boring—no wonder your sister painted me out of the picture. It's like everyone's always so bowled over by the Sun or by Venus, but the Moon, the Moon, so boring, so dull, doesn't even have her own light . . ."

It was as if she was describing my exact experience! *Poor Selene*, I thought. "I *so* know how you feel!" I said.

"Do you? How could you? You're a Zodiac Girl, and your family, well, they're all so fabulous."

"Exactly," I said. "But I'm just like you. They shine, but without them, I'm nothing. I'm little Miss Ordinary."

Selene looked at me. "You? Never. Just look at you. You're so pretty, like a caramel-colored cherub with the cutest hair. How do you get it like that?"

I felt a warm glow inside. That was the nicest thing anyone had said to me in ages. "My aunt braids it," I said. "It's called cornrow braiding when they do it close to the head like this because the braids look like sheaves of corn."

"So they do," said Selene as she looked at the top of

my head. "You should pick up some of the ends at different angles and put ribbon or colored string through it. I've seen some girls do that and it looks great."

"I like mine neat," I said.

Selene looked sad again and sighed heavily. "Sorry. I guess I don't know much about hair and beauty. That's Nessa's realm."

We sat in silence again besides her occasional sniffing. I searched my mind for something to say to make her feel better—the way she had just made me feel when she said that I was pretty and cute.

"Um . . . Selene, you know how the Moon orbits Earth?"

"Yes. Course I do, around once every twenty-nine and a half days."

"Exactly, and that's why we call a month a month! *Moon* equals *month*. How many of the other planets can say that they have words used about them? And not just any word. Not an obscure word. *Month* is a word we use all the time . . ." I said as everything I'd ever read about the Moon in Dad's books came back to me. I'd learned some of it by heart for a school assembly. "To many early civilizations, the Moon's monthly cycle was an important tool for measuring the passage of time. The Hebrew, Muslim, and Chinese calendars are *all* lunar calendars. In fact, the new moon phase is uniquely recognized as the beginning of each calendar month,

66

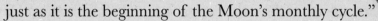

just as it is the beginning of the Moon's monthly cycle."

Selene smiled and looked more cheerful. "You're a clever little thing, aren't you?"

I felt more cheerful, too. Most people's eyes glazed over with boredom when I told them about stuff like that, but Selene looked like she was genuinely listening to me.

"And you're far from boring," I continued. "The Moon is one of my favorites because you don't just stay the same. You have all the different phases you go through. Um, let me see if I can remember them. New, new crescent, first quarter, waxing gibbous, full . . ."

"Waning gibbous, last quarter, old crescent, and back to new again," Selene added happily.

"See, that's what makes you interesting. You could never be dull, not with all that going on and words being named after you."

Suddenly she giggled. "*Month* isn't the only word named after me. Another word that has to do with the Moon is *lunar* and then *lunatic* as in crazy person. Loony."

"Oh," I said. "Um. Well, I am sure that makes you interesting, too."

And then she began to laugh. "Looo-natic," she said, drawing out the word. "That's me. Loony petunie. Lunar lunatic."

Her shoulders began to shake in a silent laugh. It was contagious. Soon my shoulders started to shake, too, and the more she laughed, the more I laughed. She said, "Looonatic," again, and then I said it. "Cra-aaaazy." It was like this wonderful private joke that just the two of us got, and the more we said it, the funnier it seemed. Selene lay back, slid down the remainder of the stairs, and landed on the second-floor landing in a heap in hysterics. I slid down after her. We couldn't stop laughing. Pat, Nessa, and Yasmin rushed out of my room to see what the noise was.

Pat took one look at us, shook her head in dismay, and said, "Lunatics," which of course set us off again, and soon we were both lying on our backs, tears running down our cheeks while Pat looked on, wondering what she'd said.

Nessa shook her head and sighed. "She's always like this when there's a full moon."

Selene smiled up at her. "Ah, but that's what makes me interesting. Right, Thebe?"

"Right, my loony friend," I said, and I put my hand up to high-five her, and she high-fived me back. Selene then coughed and tried to make her face go straight. I did the same, but then her shoulders started to shake again, and that set me off, too, and we ended up laughing so much that I got cramps.

Chapter Six

Sunshine and music

Thebe's list of things to do

1) Text Hermie, again.
2) Do homework.
3) Do weekly grocery shopping online.
   Order extra juices for all the visitors
   we've had lately. Check shampoo and
   bathroom supplies.
4) Check out exactly what is going on in my
   horoscope and what those planet people are
   supposed to be doing!

On Wednesday night, I got home to find that *another* one of the planet people was visiting. This time it was Sonny Olympus, or Mr. O., as Dad told me he liked to be called. "A big hunk," Mom said when she told me that he was in the living room. She and Dad were certainly starstruck, and so was I when I first set eyes on him. He was awesome. He was sitting on the sofa smoking a cigar and was very handsome in a white-teeth, chiseled-jaw, Hollywood-movie-star kind of way. He radiated coolness.

He beamed a hundred-watt smile at me. "So you must be Thebe? Sun in Virgo?"

"Yes. That's right," I replied and began to splutter as the smoke from his cigar made my eyes water and my chest feel tight.

Mr. O. put out his cigar immediately. "Bad habit—sorry about that. So. I suppose you have the usual Virgo allergies: wheat, dairy, pollen, and aversion to smoke?"

"Some," I said, and I crossed the room to open the window.

"Too bad. So then, little lady. What can I do for you in your Zodiac month?"

"Who, me?" I blurted. I was surprised by his question, as the other planet people who had come over this week appeared more interested in Mom and Dad than me (besides Selene), and I was starting to accept the fact that my Zodiac month was going to be a nonstarter—the stuff you read about in books but doesn't happen in real life. I turned back to him after opening the window. "Um, you could tell me where my guardian is. Hermie. He doesn't reply to anything, and he gave me a special phone, but he doesn't answer it."

"Not sure where he is, but before he left, he asked me to come over while he's gone incommunicado," said Sonny with another bright smile. "Bummer to get Mercury retrograde when you're a Zodiac Girl, but it happens sometimes. It's different for everyone, and if that's in your planetary lineup, there's not a lot you can do."

I found myself warming to him. "Yes. I guess I was hoping for an exception, seeing as I'm a Zodiac Girl this month. I wondered if I'm supposed to be doing anything or if I've done something wrong."

Sonny closed his eyes for a moment. "Okay. Now let's see if I can remember. I had a look at your chart before I came by. Uranus landed a surprise on you. Has he been over?"

"Uri, the Uranus man? Nope."

Mr. O. shrugged. "He does his own thing. The rebel of the zodiac, as you probably know. He likes to do the opposite of what people expect, so I always expect the unexpected, if you get my meaning. Now, what else? Oh yes, Mars has been in opposition to the Sun in your first house. The job of Mars is to bring up troublesome issues in the home. You have troublesome issues here, kid?"

"Sort of. Um, family stuff," I said with a glance over at Mom. I didn't want to say too much in front of her about how much I hated sharing my room with Yasmin in case she thought I was being mean. "Um . . . roommate."

"She's had to share with her cousin," Mom interjected. "It's showdown time between her parents, both Leos; neither will back down—"

"I can imagine," said Sonny.

"So Yasmin's come here for a short stay," Mom continued.

"Oh, I get it. And Thebe, you like your room neat and you like your own space, huh?" asked Sonny.

I nodded. "Dad said that we become Zodiac Girls at turning points in our lives, so I thought maybe that my having to share my room was my turning point. Like I'm supposed to learn something from it."

Mom looked at me proudly. "Thebe's a very bright girl," she said. "She catches on really fast. And she virtually runs this house single-handedly. She took over when she was ten. Said she could do a better job than the rest of us, and she has, too. She keeps everything shipshape and in order. She'll be running empires when she's older. You wait and see."

I did my best to smile modestly, but Sonny didn't look impressed at all. "Hmm. So it looks like this aspect has been sent along to stir up some family stuff," he continued. "It will pass. Everything passes. And Jupiter is prominent at the full moon at the end of the month, so that will be nice. But what's the root of this month? A difficult aspect to Saturn. There always seems to be difficult aspects to Saturn in all Zodiac Girls' charts."

"Dad said that, too. He said that Saturn is the taskmaster. The one who teaches you major lessons in life when he touches your chart. I wondered if it has to do with my cousin. I've been thinking about it a lot. I was really resistant when she got here and I'm still not happy about it, but I thought that might be the problem. I have to let go and learn to share."

"Nope. That's not it," said Sonny.

"Why not?"

"It's never that simple with Saturn. You've just told me exactly what you need to do with that situation. You've figured it out, learned your lesson, and it sounds like you've given yourself some good advice. Nope, the lesson Saturn has to teach you is more subtle, deeper."

"So what is it? Dr. Cronus was here the other day, but he hardly even spoke to me. Can you help me?"

Sonny beamed again. "Maybe, maybe not. See, being a Zodiac Girl, it's all about how you run with it. You can't have expectations because it's different for everyone. Now then, how about you put on some music, we kick off our shoes, and sit back and relax?"

Kick off my shoes? Relax? Is this man insane? I asked myself. It wasn't the time. I'd just gotten home from school and had a list of things to do. "Can't. I have homework to do and—"

"You can do it later," said Mom, and she kicked off her shoes and looked coyly at Sonny.

He got up, took off his shoes, pulled a CD from his pocket, and put it into the CD player. "Summer chill-out sounds. Just the thing for an evening like this when it's wet outside. I brought it especially for you. It's my favorite," he said. "Now let's close the blinds—light a candle, Mrs. Battye, if you would—and let's all lay back and enjoy being in this wonderful room."

Our living room was the Scorpio-themed room. I called it the Goth room because it was painted blood-red, with spooky paintings of dark angels and crows on the wall and a huge silver candelabra in the fireplace—very dramatic. It wasn't my favorite room in the house partly because the paintings made me feel uncomfortable, but also because the heavy velvet curtains were a dust trap and they always set off my allergy when I cleaned in there. Mom got up and lit a candle in the fireplace.

"Okay, let's all lay on the floor," said Sonny.

"Can I be excused?" I asked. "I really do have stuff to do, a pile of homework, and—"

"Thebe's an A student," said Mom. "We never have to remind her to do her homework like we do our other daughter."

"Indeed," said Sonny. "Well, even A students need some time off. What do you do to relax, kid?"

"Um . . . play on the computer. I don't know.

Crosswords sometimes. Word games. Chess. Surfing the Internet. I like staying busy. That's how I relax."

"Okaaaaay," said Sonny. "Yes. Good. It's good to work, excellent, but you've got to have balance. Light and dark. Yin and yang. Sweet and sour. So come on, kick back."

Mom made a face as if to tell me to do as I was told, so I took off my shoes and lay back on the floor.

"Hit the play button, Estella, my friend," said Sonny, and he lay down on the rug. "Ah, one, two, three, let's be in the moment and go with the music."

The swell of a hundred violins filled the air. I closed my eyes and began to listen.

I've never done anything like this before, I thought. *Just wait till I tell Rachel. Although I have listened to music, but only when it's been on in the background. Oops, have an itchy foot.* I sat up and scratched my left foot and then lay back down. *Wonder if Mom and Sonny have their eyes closed.* I couldn't resist, so I peeked. Yes, they both looked very peaceful. *Close my eyes. Okay. Come on, Thebe. Relax. Wonder how long it will take to do my French homework tonight. And I have to prepare for my history project, too. And I suppose I'll have to attempt ice-skating, although I can't imagine I'll ever manage to do it. Oops, have an itch on my head.* I scratched my forehead.

"Stop twitching, Thebe," said Mom. "She's so fidgety, Sonny. Can't ever sit still. Even when she's watching TV, her foot twitches."

"Just listen to the music," said Sonny in a dreamy voice. "Let it wash over you."

My back hurt. It was hard down on the floor, even if there was a rug underneath us. I made an effort to listen to the music, though. It was really nice. Soothing, but my mind was soon off again. It was crazy. Like there was a whole pile of people in there commenting on what was happening and making lists of things to do. Lists? That's what I should be doing. Making my list of things to do. And that wasn't the only list I made. I had notebooks filled with lists. Lists of my favorite music, my favorite movies. Lists of foods I liked and foods I didn't. My favorite people. Favorite books. Lists of my worries. My pet hates. My goals. I liked lists. They made me feel safe and secure. And I liked checking off the jobs on the "things to do" ones. Check. Check. Check. Done. There was always a nice feeling of having achieved something. That was how I relaxed. By writing lists and by getting things done, not by lying around in the dark.

"You're not listening to the music, Thebe," said Sonny. "Relax. Chill. Let it all go."

I made my mind go back to the music, but I couldn't stay with it. My mind was too active. I liked Sonny, but he wasn't much use. I opened my eyes and looked up at the dark ceiling.

Yasmin popped her head around the door, surveyed the scene, and made a disapproving face. "Crazy," she declared and shut the door.

For once I had to agree with her. Relaxation. Who'd have ever thought it was such hard work?

Chapter Seven

Desperately seeking someone!

Another week went by and still no sign of Hermie. Not an e-mail, not a call, not a text message on my Zodiac phone—which I checked regularly. My month as a Zodiac Girl was almost half over and nothing had happened. At least not for me. Mom and Dad were having a merry old time entertaining their new planet pals, most of whom had been over while I was at school. At least one of them was also over most evenings, hanging out, having drinks, and chatting in the study or sitting out on the patio. Our backyard was looking lovely at the moment, with tumbles of flowers cascading down over the trellis. It's usually my favorite time of year, as all the roses, clematis, and wisteria suddenly come into bloom, but this year I couldn't appreciate it. The Zodiac thing was bugging me. Not that anyone seemed that bothered about it except for me. Pat and Yasmin were happy, as they appeared to have bonded with Nessa, who was often found in either my room or Pat's after school talking hair, makeup, and nails while they listened to music. Even Selene, who I thought would have been more sensitive to my case, was over one night having a long conference call with Mom and Auntie Maggie and Uncle Norrece about how to fix their marriage. Seemed like the whole family was benefiting from being with the planets, except for me. I had never felt so left out of anything in my whole life. I was starting to feel more and more upset about it all, to the point that I could hardly sleep, as my mind went over and over what I thought should or *could* have been happening.

One night after yet another pathetic attempt at ice-skating, I decided that I couldn't face going home again only to feel like the odd one out. Instead I decided to go into Osbury and see what the planets got up to when they weren't hanging out with my relatives at Zodiac Lodge. I especially wanted to see if I could find Hermie.

I explained my plan to Rachel during the afternoon break at school on Friday. "If the mountain won't come to Muhammad, Muhammad must go to the mountain. You coming?"

"Wouldn't miss it. I love mountain climbing," she said, and then when she saw my blank reaction, she added, "That was a joke, Thebe."

"Sorry," I said. "Course. Very funny. Sorry. Been a little distracted lately."

"You can say that again."

"Been a little distracted lately," I repeated to show that I hadn't totally lost my sense of humor.

Rachel rolled her eyes. "Okay. Just let me call Mom and let her know I'll be late coming home," she said.

At least I have one friend in this world, I thought as Rachel spoke to her mom. It wouldn't be a long journey—we had to take our school bus to the bottom of the hill and then change for the number 73 bus, which would take us straight there. Easy as pie. It would take around 40 minutes.

"What do you do to relax?" I asked Rachel once we'd gotten onto the second bus after school.

"Watch TV," she replied. "Read. Sometimes I like to just lie on my bed and look up at the sky through the window and let my mind wander wherever it wants. Why do you ask?"

"No reason. Um . . . do I strike you as a relaxed kind of person?"

Rachel burst out laughing.

"Why is that funny?" I asked.

"Because you are one of life's doers, not one of life's dreamers. Knowing you, if you were going to relax, you'd have to make a list of how you were going to go about it first, with a schedule saying when and for how long."

Not a bad idea, I thought, and I made a mental note to do just that. I could put relaxation on my list of things to do and include it with my school schedule. I liked to highlight my different subject areas in different-colored markers. I enjoyed doing that almost as much as making my lists. I'd mark each subject in a different color. Green for geography, blue for history, and so on. Yellow could be for relaxation. I had two separate sheets. One for the schedule at school and one for my homework schedule. That way, I could see clearly exactly where I was up to and what needed to be done and what time was spare. Then I realized that Rachel was joking.

"I can relax. Really I can. It's just that everyone has their own way of doing it."

"Exactly," said Rachel, but she didn't look convinced.

We didn't talk about it anymore because the bus had reached its last stop. We had arrived in Osbury.

Luckily for us, the rain that had been threatening earlier had blown over, and the afternoon had brightened. We got off and surveyed the area. It was a small town with a patch of grass in front of the bus stop, a church at the end of a little park, a bush of white roses by the town hall, and a row of stores across the street.

"Where to?" asked Rachel.

I pointed to the stores. "Let's start there first."

We made our way across the street and looked at the stores. There were the usual: drugstore, convenience store, thrift store, hardware store, grocery store.

"Doesn't look like the kind of place where planets would live," said Rachel.

I was about to agree with her when I spotted a deli. "Ha," I said. "Look over there. I bet that's the deli Jupiter owns. Dad told me that's what he does. Look, it's called Europa, and Europa is one of the four moons of Jupiter. Io, Europa, Ganymede, and Callisto."

We went over for a closer look. It seemed like any other deli. Tables, chairs, a counter at the back. A big notice on the door said, "CLOSED."

"Well, it is four-thirty," said Rachel.

"I guess. But most places don't close until six or so."

"Maybe he's on vacation. Hey," said Rachel when we walked on and she spotted a beauty salon, "didn't you say Nessa owns a beauty salon?"

I nodded. "And I bet that's it," I said when I noticed that it was called Pentangle. "That would be appropriate for Venus. A pentangle is a five-pointed star, and that is often associated with Venus."

"Why?"

"I think that Venus makes a pentangle star shape as it travels around the Sun," I replied. "Let's go in and see if anyone knows anything about Hermie."

We went up to the door, but it was clear that no one was there either. The blinds were down, and on the door was a sign like the one at Europa. CLOSED.

"And I bet I know exactly where she is, too," I said.

"Your house?"

I nodded. "Along with the others. Not to see me,

though. It was last week that my moon was conjunct with Venus. From what I've been able to see, there are no encounters with her this week or next, but then, I might be wrong. If only Hermie was here, he could explain." I pointed to another storefront toward the end of the row. "And there's the Internet café Dad talked about. It's also a magic shop."

"That's run by the Uranus planet man, isn't it?"

"I guess so. At least it is when it's open," I said as I noticed another CLOSED sign. "What is it with this place? It's like a ghost town. Doesn't anyone work around here?"

Rachel pointed to a fish-and-chips restaurant. "That's bound to be open. Let's go in there. I'm starving."

"I wouldn't even bother checking," I said when I saw the name of the place. Poseidon. "Poseidon's another name for Neptune. He'll be over having a drink with Dad." Sure enough, when we got close to see, there was a CLOSED sign on the door. "Apparently some of them are at our house during the day, too, having lunch, playing cards."

"You sound upset, Thebe," said Rachel, and she linked her arm through mine. "Come on. I'll buy you some candy to cheer you up."

I tried to smile, but she was right. I was upset. I couldn't help it, but I was getting more and more angry about the fact that everyone in the world seemed to be having a good time in my Zodiac month except me.

Rachel bought candy for me and some chips for her, and then we walked up and down the street a few times and looked in all the windows. There was no sign of Hermie or any of the planet people. I even asked a couple of people in various stores if they'd seen Hermie or knew an office or building called Mercury Communications. Most people knew who he was, but no one could tell me where to find him.

"On vacation, I think, dear," said a young red-haired man at the drugstore.

"Haven't seen him around lately," said an elderly Indian man at the convenience store. "He often disappears a couple of times a year. Goes off on that bike of his."

"I heard he likes to go to a spa resort," said an old lady in the thrift store. "One of those rest, get pampered, relax, and recharge type of places. Good for him, eh?"

After a good half hour, we had to catch the bus, as Rachel had to be back home for dinner. I got onboard feeling disappointed. We found seats at the back, and as we sat down, my Zodiaphone beeped that there was a message. My spirits rose in an instant as I glanced down.

"Merwanna peranna, oogie boogie blurh," read the message.

Rachel looked over my shoulders. "Is that planet speak?" she asked. "Do we need a dictionary to interpret it?"

I shook my head. "No. It's just typical of the type of thing that can happen when Mercury is retrograde. Remember? Mercury retrograde means garbled messages. Miscommunication."

Rachel cracked up laughing. "Excellent," she said. "Because you can't get more garbled than that. Merwanna peranna, oogie boogie blurh."

I wished I could have laughed along with her, but it didn't strike me as funny. It was just another disappointment in my "special" month.

Chapter Eight

Preparation!

"You making one of your lists?" asked Rachel when she found me sitting outside the gym just before assembly on the following Friday.

"Yep. Big night tonight," I said as I showed her my notebook.

<u>Thebe's list of things to do</u>

1) Hallway: Mars area. Remove shoes and coats not being used. Make sure there are flowers.

2) Living room: Pluto area. Needs to be dusted.

3) Study: Mercury area. Put books and magazines into neat piles.

4) Dining room: Jupiter area. Dust and polish. Shine glasses and silverware.

5) Kitchen: Sun area. Clear and clean all surfaces.

6) Mom and Dad's bedroom: Uranus area. Pick up all discarded clothes.

7) Bathroom: Neptune area. Wash towels

and put out new soaps.

8) My room: Venus area. Clean my side.
9) Pat's room: ex-Moon area. No entry.
10) Spare room: Saturn area. Keep door firmly shut.
11) Confirm food and fruit punch.

"Long list. Big night? What's happening?" she asked.

"Mom's asked all the planet people over for dinner, and I've decided that what I need to do is organize all of them," I said.

"Organize them? But why?" she asked as she looked over my list again.

"I think they're all spaced out. Seriously. Disorganized. They've forgotten what they're supposed to be doing. I think they need a secretary or an assistant or someone to do their schedules and sort them out."

Rachel looked doubtful. "I don't know. I mean, they're the planet people and you're the Zodiac Girl. Aren't they supposed to be telling you what to do?"

"That's just it. They're not telling me *anything*. I get home most nights to find one or two of them there lounging around in Dad's study or lazing in the yard— like, doing *nothing*. Anyone would think that they're on vacation. I told you about the other night when Sonny was over. I mean, lying around listening to music?

Excuse me, but what a waste of time that was. And Selene, although she's very nice, she needs to get a grip. Way too emotional. Crying one minute. Laughing the next. And Nessa, hanging out doing people's nails. I mean, puhleese, has she forgotten who she is?"

Rachel still looked anxious. "I don't know, Thebe. It sounds to me like they feel at home at your place, and who can blame them? It must be like their dream house."

"Maybe, but surely they have planet work to do?"

"Yeah, but even planet people deserve some time off, don't you think? And maybe how they choose to relax is their business, their choice. I mean, you can't control the planets, can you?"

"I'm not going to try to *control* them!"

"Well, you know what you're like."

"What do you mean? What am I like?"

"Well, you can be a bit . . . bossy sometimes."

"Me? Bossy? No way. Sit up straight, Rachel."

Rachel immediately sat up.

"That was a joke, Rachel."

"Oh! Course. But you do like to do things your own way."

"I like to do things *right*, that's all. Like at home, if I didn't tell everyone what to do, we'd never eat or have clean clothes. And Mom and Dad love it that I color coordinate their wardrobes. It makes it so easy for them to find what they're looking for. You should try it. All the dark colors together, all the whites in one place, all Dad's Hawaiian shirts together. It looks better, too. So I run the household? That's not controlling. That's being *organized*. That's all. And this is supposed to my special month. I want to do it *right*."

Rachel shrugged her shoulders. "It's your call. So what are you going to do?"

"We'll have dinner, and then with them all there I'm hoping to make some plans—"

"And some lists," Rachel added.

I got the feeling that she was making fun of me a little. She likes to do that sometimes when she thinks I'm going into what she calls one of my "I'm-going-to-take-over-the-world" phases.

"Yeah, lists. I want to synchronize dates in the calendar this month with those highlighted as important in my birth chart. I want to make sure that if any planet person has a part to play, they don't forget or ignore me. Like Saturn features strongly this month, but he was over the other night and barely glanced my way. He was too busy with his nose in one of Dad's books. I also think he wasn't very happy when he found out that the Saturn room was being used for storage—but at least he didn't cry about it like Selene did when she discovered that Pat had painted her out."

Rachel started laughing. "Poor planet people. Sounds like they're in for a scolding."

"No way. Just a . . . reminder."

Rachel squeezed my arm. "I'm only teasing, Thebe. And you're right. Some people do need organizing, and you're *just* the person to do it! So tell me what you've got planned for the dinner."

"The food part's easy. Auntie Nikkya will cater, as usual."

"Great," said Rachel. "So what else?"

"I'm going to seat them at the same angles as they are in my chart."

"Angles in your chart? You know I don't understand astrology like you do. What do you mean?"

"In a birth chart, depending on where the planets are at the time of your birth, they sit at different angles to one another. Like, they can be conjunct—that means within an eight-degree orb of each other, sextile—that means sixty degrees apart, square—that means ninety degrees apart, trine—that means one hundred and twenty degrees apart, opposite—that means one hundred and eighty degrees apart."

Rachel held up her palm and said in a robot-type flat voice, "Information overload, information overload. Brain's going to explode, brain's going to explode. What you're saying is that astrology is very complicated, right? Least it is to me. It's like you're talking Greek when you go on about trines and sextiles and stuff."

I laughed. "I guess. I wouldn't worry about it, Rach. It just means that I'm going to seat them in the right alignments."

"Can I come? I'll help you set up, but you have to tell me what to do in plain English, not astrogobbledygook."

"Absolutely. I already asked Mom, and she said you could."

Rachel clapped her hands. "Great. Oh, but, oh God, what if I can't remember who they all are?"

"I've thought of that," I said and ripped a page out of my notebook. "Here. I did this for you. It's a list of who's who so that you can come prepared."

She took the list and glanced at it.

Sun: Sonny Olympus (or Mr. O.). Actor. Big hunk.

Moon: Selene Luna. Counselor.

Mars: Mario Ares. Ex-Marine. Teaches self-defense.

Venus: Nessa. Runs a beauty salon and classes about how to find your inner goddess.

Pluto: P. J. Vlasaova. Interior designer. Goth.

Uranus: Uri. Runs a magic shop and Internet café.

Neptune: Captain John Dory. Runs a fish-and-chips restaurant.

Mercury: Hermie. Motorcycle messenger.

Saturn: Dr. Cronus. Headmaster.

Jupiter. Joe Joeve. Deli owner.

"Thanks. That will help me remember," she said. "You really do think of everything."

"I try to," I said.

"What about the antistars? Yasmin and Pat?"

"As soon as they heard about it, they were both calling around trying to find a friend's house to go to. I hope they do. In fact, I can't wait until Yasmin leaves for good. It's been awful sharing my room with her. She treats me like I'm her least favorite person on the planet, which is so not fair. I did try in the beginning to make an effort to get along with her, but she hasn't tried at all."

Rachel sighed. "Teenagers can be difficult."

"*We're* teenagers, Rach," I said. "In case you hadn't noticed."

"You know what I mean. Older ones. They think they know everything. My policy is to pretend they don't exist. So. Are all the planets coming?"

"Except for Hermie. Seven o'clock is kickoff. Be there or be square."

"Or conjunct or whatever," said Rachel.

I smacked her arm lightly. "Ha-ha, very funny. Now shut up or I'll write you another list."

Preparations were already under way when I got home, in plenty of time to help set the table. Mom was up in her room buzzing with excitement, and she had around eight outfits on her bed.

"I don't know what to wear," she said with a sigh as

she tried on a blue dress and then turned to look at herself in the mirror. "Bit much? Does my butt look big in this?"

"No, you look great. All the outfits are lovely," I said as I got out my notebook and consulted one of my lists. "Um . . . just checking that you know what to do tonight."

"Yes. Absolutely. Hand out the drinks, right?"

"Right."

"And you said you're going to make up a drinks menu for our guests to choose from."

"I've done it," I said. I'd spent the whole previous evening researching cocktail names on the Internet and then adapting them for Auntie Nikkya's alcohol-free fruit punch. "Want to have a look?"

Mom took the list and glanced at it.

*** Menu for the Stars ***

Jungle Jupiter

Saturn Surprise

Pluto Punch

Uranus Um Bongo

Venus Sunset

Mars Mojito

Moonbeam Margarita

Screaming Sun

Neptune Nightcap

Hermie Highball

"Fabulous, baby. You're a star," she said.

"No, they are," I joked. "Rachel and I will be taking coats."

"What time is Nikkya* bringing the food and the punch?"

"Just before seven. All we have to do is pour the drinks and then heat up the food as usual. She's making ten varieties of her punch with a different fruit juice in each so that each planet can have their own."

"Excellent," said Mom. "I think they're going to like it. I checked and none of them drink alcohol, so no need to provide any of that."

"Why don't they drink alcohol?" I asked.

"Mr. O. said they used to drink nectar of the gods and nothing compares to that, but then again, they haven't tasted Nikkya's fruit punch."

"They're going to love it. I *so* want tonight to be perfect, don't you?"

Mom nodded. "It will be."

"When will Dad be back?"

"Just in time. He's in the city doing a prerecording for next week's show and meeting with that ice-skating lady. How are you doing with your skating?"

"Oh, making progress," I lied. I didn't want to ruin the evening by telling her how useless I was at it.

Luckily, she was much too involved with the preparations for dinner. "Benjie said he'd heard back from everyone besides—"

"Hermie," I finished for her.

She nodded. "And Mars and Pluto can't make it after all. Mario teaches a self-defense class he couldn't get out of, and P. J., Pluto, had a house makeover to do, but don't worry, hon, not many girls can say that they have a guest list like yours tonight, even if a few of them are missing."

I felt slightly annoyed that they had come over and met Mom and Dad during the day while I was out, yet they couldn't rearrange things to get to our special dinner. But I was determined that nothing was going to spoil our night. "I know. I'm not going to get upset about it. I think we're going to have a lot of fun, even if a couple are missing."

"That's the attitude," said Mom.

Next door in my room, Yasmin was on the phone to one of her friends. "I am so out of here tonight," she said, with no attempt to keep her voice down when I walked in. "My weirdo relatives have an even weirder bunch of people coming over."

Good, I thought, *fine by me*. I didn't want her around with her killjoy attitude. I went and played on my computer while she finished her call. I wrote out the guest list and then made neat borders around each of the names. After a while, I became aware that Yasmin was watching me over my shoulder.

"What are you doing?" she asked a few moments later.

"Place names," I said as I scrolled down so that she didn't see too much. I didn't want her making fun of me.

She scrutinized the screen. "Neptune. Venus. Jupiter . . ." she read. "Are you having a costume party?"

"Sort of," I said. I didn't want to get into who they really were in case she asked too many questions and then realized that my guardian had gone missing. She'd love to rub my face in that.

"Your family is crazy," she said.

I smiled back. I could have said something about hers but bit my lip and agreed. "Yeah, I guess. Where are you going?"

"Sleepover at a friend's. And Pat's coming, too."

Yippee, I thought. *I get my room back for one night, and maybe Nessa will pay some attention to me, too.* "Oh well, have a good time," I said.

Ten minutes later, we heard a car horn beep outside, and then she and Pat were gone. I couldn't have planned it better. I focused on my computer and set about looking at images from the Web of the various planets. My idea was to print out little place cards for all of them so that they'd know exactly where to sit. When I'd finished with the place names, I printed out my last-minute "to do" list.

<u>Thebe's list of things to do</u>
1) Lay out outfit.
2) Shower and change.
3) Check food is all there.
4) Set table.
5) Set place mats according to my horoscope.
6) Light candles for atmosphere.
7) Have CDs ready for background music.
8) Put the answering machine on so that there are no interruptions.

So there wouldn't be a full set of planets—at least the rest of the plan was going beautifully. This evening was going to be the best ever. I couldn't wait.

Chapter Nine

Star-studded dinner

At seven o'clock, the doorbell rang, and I went down to answer it. It was Rachel, right on time, and she looked really pretty in a dusty pink top and rose pink skirt. She had also put on star-shaped silver earrings for the occasion.

"Perfect," I said.

"You look great, too," she said. "Star child."

I gave her a twirl. I'd put on my best dress. I'd gotten it for Auntie Francelle's wedding last year. It was red with a halter neck, and the material was covered in tiny silver stars. I also made sure I was wearing the necklace that Hermie had given me.

"So set me to work," said Rachel. "Where are we going to be?"

I showed her into the dining room. "In here."

"Jupiter room, right?" she asked. "I keep forgetting which is which. I could probably use one of your lists to remind me."

"You won't need one. We won't go into any of the rooms besides this one and the kitchen. Jupiter is the planet of merriment and expansion, so Dad thought it seemed fitting that the dining room was done in his honor. Jupiter was also known in Roman times as the king of the gods."

"Awesome. Has he been here yet?"

I nodded. "Earlier in the week. Not that he took much notice of me, though."

"What's he like?"

"Big and jolly with a black mustache and very approachable for someone who's the king of the gods, but then again, they're all playing it down. I guess they have to or else they'd attract too much attention."

"They have to go undercover, like cops on a job."

"Something like that. Remember, we saw Jupiter's deli in Osbury."

"Yes, Europa. Named after one of the four moons of Jupiter, you said."

"That's it. You're getting it," I replied as Rachel looked at the painting depicting Jupiter on the wall. It was another one of Auntie Francelle's works and showed a majestic bearded man on a throne. In the background was a centaur—half man and half horse—which is the symbol for Sagittarius.

"Luckily the dining table is round," I said as I began to set out the place names, "the same shape as a birth chart, so I can get people in just about the same positions as they were in the sky at the time of my birth."

"Right. Whatever," said Rachel as the phone in the hall rang and went into answering mode. "Where should I sit?"

"Over on the left, next to me. I'll put Mom, Dad, you, and me over there—that should work, as most of the planets in my chart are over on one side, so I can put them all together. Except for the Sun, that's across from Saturn. See, there are a few houses in my chart that are empty. Dad said that's because I'm an old soul. He says you can always tell an old soul because they have all the planets piled in one place, as if they have a last lesson to learn in one area of their life. I'm still not sure what that is for me. I was hoping to find out this month."

Rachel had a mystified expression on her face. "I have absolutely no idea what you're talking about," she said, "but I don't care. I'm just happy to be here."

I handed her some matches. "Fine. In that case, you just light some candles."

"That I can do," she said as the phone rang again. "Should I get that?"

I shook my head. "I put the answering machine on. My Zodiac phone is on in case Hermie or any of the planet people needs to get through."

The first guest to arrive was Dr. Cronus.

"Drinks are in the Jupiter room," said Mom, directing him into the dining room. She looked lovely and had settled for a classy green silk pants suit with a gold necklace and earrings. Dr. Cronus looked like he'd also made an effort for the evening. He had on a nicer-than-usual tweed suit and vest, and he was wearing a red bow tie with tiny stars and planets on it. He bowed stiffly and followed Mom.

"He doesn't look like a barrel of laughs," whispered Rachel.

"He's not. He's a headmaster," I said.

"Eek," she said as we went into the kitchen to finish the drinks. They were all set out in their pitchers and labeled so that I could see which one was which, and the room smelled wonderful with the scent of fruit and mixed spices.

Next to arrive were Nessa and Sonny. This time, she really did look like a goddess. She was wearing a white off-the-shoulder dress, and her hair was up, with little diamante stars arranged through it. Mr. O. had on a black suit and bow tie, as if he was going to a very fancy ball.

Rachel's eyes almost popped out of her head. "They are the most glamorous people I have ever seen in my whole life," she whispered after we'd taken Nessa's wrap.

"Very Oscars," I agreed.

Selene arrived on her own. She also had dressed up and was wearing a silver silk top with a long, shimmery green skirt. Around her neck she had a moon necklace, with matching earrings in her ears. "It's so generous of you to have this evening for us," she said to Mom. "We so rarely get the chance to get together like this."

"Our pleasure," said Mom, ushering her down the hallway to join the others.

"Is she the Moon lady?" asked Rachel.

Selene overheard and turned back to her. "I am, and I do believe you're Thebe's friend."

Rachel nodded. She seemed to have lost her tongue and had become shy, like someone meeting the president.

"This is Rachel," I said. "And her sign is Cancer."

"Which means that the Moon is your ruling planet," said Selene with an encouraging smile.

"Yes," whispered Rachel.

"Come on," said Selene. "Let's you and me go and get to know each other. Us moonstruck types have to stick together."

Rachel glanced at me, and I nodded. Okay, so it was someone else about to have a good time with one of the planet people in *my* month, but I didn't mind it being Rachel. She was my best friend, and I was glad to share some of the excitement with her.

"Please come through," I said. I could barely contain

my excitement, and I knew that Mom and Rachel felt the same. As our guests began to fill the dining room, Mom caught my eye and then did a little tap dance on the spot as if to say she was having a great time.

By 7:45, Captain John and Joe had arrived and were in the dining room with the others. They were also in their best clothes, and I stood at the door and marveled at how sophisticated they all looked.

"So who's missing?" asked Mom.

I did a quick count around. "Hermie—no surprise there—Mario and P. J., who we knew about, and Uranus."

"Uranus? Hmm," Mr. O. said. "He may show up, but you know what Uranus is like. The planet of the unexpected. He'll come in his own time, in his own way, and it will probably be in some kind of extraordinary or eccentric fashion."

We decided to give Uri and Hermie a few more minutes while the others mingled and drank Auntie Nikkya's fruit punch. When each of them saw the names of the drinks on the menu that I'd put out, they seemed genuinely delighted.

I poured Mr. O. a large glass. "It's mostly juice," I said as he finished the glass in one gulp.

"Hmm, that's good."

"Would you like another one?"

Mr. O. nodded, and I refilled his glass and then went

around refilling the others and making sure that everyone had what they wanted. It was always the same when we served Auntie Nikkya's punch. Everyone loved it.

"You can tell that they feel comfortable here," said Rachel. After half an hour, we refilled glasses and passed around nuts, olives, and chips again. She looked down at her empty pitcher of Neptune Nightcap. "We might need more of this one soon."

I nodded and followed her into the kitchen and looked on the counter where the pitchers were. Most of them were almost empty bar Hermie's.

"Everyone must be really thirsty," I said as I picked up a jug of Saturn Surprise to take into the dining room.

Dad came through with another empty pitcher. "Need a hand?" he asked.

"Drinks need refilling," I said. "They seem to really like them."

Dad winked. "They do indeed. It's that special Caribbean flavor that Nikkya creates. No one does it like her."

At that moment, Mom came through to join us and overheard him. "Do you know what her special ingredient is?"

I shook my head. "I can taste coconut and banana, but I'm not sure what else."

"Spices, cinnamon, nutmeg," said Mom, "but besides that, it's her secret."

"No worries," said Dad, and he picked up a pitcher of Mars Mojito to take back in to the guests. "It's a hit, and that's all that matters."

We followed Mom back into the dining room, and I glanced around. Everyone seemed happy, chatting away, laughing. Okay, so Captain John Dory's face looked slightly flushed and Dr. Cronus's cheeks were almost beet red and the noise level in the room had gone up a couple of decibels, but these were good signs that the evening was going well.

Just at that moment, the phone in the hall rang again.

"Get that, will you, Thebe, baby?" asked Mom. "It's been ringing all night—just in case it's Pat needing something."

I went into the hall and picked up. It was Auntie Nikkya. She sounded upset. "Oh, thank God, Thebe. Have your guests arrived? What's happening there?"

"Yes, just about everyone's here. Why?"

"I've been trying all night to get through, but no one was picking up—"

"Does it have something to do with the food?" I interrupted. "Something I have to do?"

"No. No. Just . . . okay, Nikkya, take a breath," she told herself. "Thebe, have you served the drinks yet?"

"Um . . . some." At the other end, Auntie Nikkya let out a loud groan. "Oh *noooooooooooooo*."

"Why? What's wrong?"

105

"Honey. Oh God, oh Lord, get them to drink some water or eat something or preferably go and lie down somewhere."

I felt a knot in my stomach twist tight. "What's wrong with the drinks?"

"Honey. It's in the punch. Your dad sent me over a message that your guests were allergic, but . . . oh Lord, it must have fallen behind the coffeemaker, and I only just found it on a Post-it note. No honey. Oh Lord, that punch is full of honey; it gives that special sweetness. Are your guests okay?"

"They seem to be," I said. "Listen, I'll call Dad now."

I dashed into the dining room and pulled Dad out into the hall and quickly filled him in on the situation. He said a few words to Auntie Nikkya and then sat down heavily on the hall chair.

"But what does it mean, Dad?" I asked.

"Oh Lord, baby girl, it's a disaster. I looked it up in one of my books after Hermie warned us that day when he first came over, which is why I sent the message over to Nikkya."

"Yes, but don't forget with Mercury retrograde . . ."

Dad nodded. "Expect miscommunication, misunderstandings, messages to go astray. I should have known and double-checked. Oh Lord, what are we going to do?"

"But what will happen to them? Will they get sick?

106

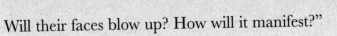

Will their faces blow up? How will it manifest?"

Dad sighed. "There is nothing more intoxicating for them. One drop and they'll be tipsy. Two drops and they'll be dancing on the furniture. Three drops and . . . oh Lord, oh my, you get the picture?"

"Think so. Um. I'd better go warn Mom."

I raced into the dining room, where I quickly filled in Mom and Rachel.

Mom glanced around. "I think that maybe we should serve food, get some solids in them, and *quickly*," she whispered.

"Good idea," said Dad. "The effects are beginning to show."

I glanced around. They were all looking bright eyed now. I picked up a fork from the table and hit it on the side of one of the glasses. "Dinner will be served in a moment if you'd like to take your places," I announced.

"What, already?" said Nessa. A few strands of her hair had come down, and she was looking slightly cross-eyed. "No. Let's boogie first."

"Yes, let's dance," agreed Selene, who was also looking dazed. "Put on some music."

"Yes, yes, music," said Dad, and he went over to the CD player and read out all of the titles he could that had anything to do with the stars or the sky. "What tickles your fancy? Starlight Express? Moon River? Music from The Planets?"

Everyone started laughing hysterically, as if he was the funniest comedian who had ever lived. *It wasn't that funny*, I thought as I watched tears roll down Joe's cheeks. Finally, Dad picked a disco CD and put it on. Within moments, they were all dancing away merrily. All had their own style—Selene was doing a dreamy dance with swaying arms, Dad and Nessa started jiving, Dr. Cronus put his arms around Mom and began waltzing, Joe did some Greek dancing, and Captain John Dory attempted to do Irish river dancing, which made Rachel crack up laughing. When the second track started up, Nessa called out, "Make a line, let's do the hokey pokey. Let's do the conga."

Dad looked over, shrugged, and held up his hands as if to say, *What can we do?*

"Great party," said Mr. O. with a grin as they formed a line, and off they went around the room, each one with their hands on the hips of the person in front of them.

"If you can't beat 'em, join 'em," said Mom.

"Just what I was thinking," said Dad. "Maybe it will be all right after all." And he and Mom joined the line.

"You put your left leg in, your left leg out, in, out, in, out, shake it all about . . ." they sang together. Selene and Dr. Cronus were looking a little shaky, and he was still flushed in the face, but that didn't stop them.

"I think it's going to be okay," Rachel said with an anxious glance at them. "They're only dancing."

I told myself to relax. *Only dancing. Only dancing. Relax. Relax.* But my inner knot was getting more and more tangled as it twisted and turned inside of me. *Oops,* I thought as I watched my esteemed guests and realized that they were behaving like a bunch of drunken relatives at a wedding.

Rachel turned to me and grinned when Nessa bumped into a cabinet and Mr. O. almost tripped over a chair. "There's nothing we can do, Thebe, except join them and dance."

She ran over to the end of the line, put her hands on the last person, who was Joe, and off they all danced, out into the hall and up the stairs. Unsure what to do, I ran after them.

"Come on, join in," called Rachel.

"Yes, come on, Thebe," urged Mom, who seemed to have let go of any anxieties and was having the time of her life.

"Come on, Zodiac Girl," said Mr. O.

And then with Nessa leading, they started singing. "Olé, olé, olé, olé, vum vum, vum vum. Olé, olé, olé, olé, leg in, leg out, shake it all about . . ."

I tried to get Mom or Dad's attention. Dinner was ready. It needed to be served or else it would burn. And there was a thumping on the wall and the muffled sound of Mrs. Janson next door yelling, "Keep that noise down!"

No one took any notice as Nessa continued to lead the conga line. I stood on a chair and yelled at the top of my voice, "DINNER!"

The line stopped, and everyone turned to look at me.

"We *need* to eat," I said. "*Sit* at the table."

"Tee-hee. Zodiac Girl hath spoken," said Joe. "We must obey."

"Yes, you must come and sit down. NOW!" I said. Joe started giggling.

"And *you*, you're supposed to be the king of the gods," I said. "You should be setting an example, not acting like a troublemaker."

Selene and Nessa cracked up laughing. "Jupiter, you're a troublemaker," Selene said with a snicker.

Joe looked put out and glanced around at the others. Then his face cracked a huge smile. "This is like the parties we used to have on Mount Olympus in the old days. Remember? Ah, those were the days. Come on, let's do the Zorba dance." He summoned everyone into the position for Greek dancing—a line where they stood side to side with their arms alongside the shoulders of the people next to them.

"No, NO, time to eat. You need some food," I urged as I climbed down off the chair.

"We *need* to dance," said Selene, and she looked as if she might burst into tears at any moment. "Nobody

110

dances enough anymore. Come on, let's be butterflies." And she started flapping her arms like wings. *She really is loony*, I thought as I watched her.

"That's true, need to dance," chorused Mom and Nessa, and for a moment they looked sad, but then they acted like butterflies, too.

"Your mom is great," said Rachel, and she also began to be a butterfly.

"Put on *Zorba the Greek* music," said Joe. "I'm the king, so I get to say what dance we do. In fact, no, forget the Zorba—let's do the plate-smashing dance. Mrs. Battye, where are your plates?"

"NOOOOOOOOOO," I said as a picture of a kitchen full of smashed plates flashed through my mind. I climbed back up on the chair. "All of you BEHAVE. This is terrible. Have you forgotten who you are? No. You either do as I say or you leave now and NO DINNER and *definitely* no dessert, and Aunt Nikkya has made coconut ice cream especially!"

The planet people and Mom and Dad hung their heads and looked at the floor like a bunch of naughty five-year-olds—but it had done the trick. They took their seats according to the table plan.

"She's very strict," Dr. Cronus whispered to Joe as he wobbled past and sat down.

"I know," said Joe. "Scary."

Serving the food was simple enough, and between

Rachel, Mom, and I, it was on the table in an instant. Everyone oohed and aahed and said it smelled wonderful. Auntie Nikkya was a great cook, and as everyone settled down to eat, albeit shakily on a few people's parts, it appeared that the evening was back on track and was going to be a success after all.

"Welcome," said Dad. "Eat. Enjoy."

It was then that I noticed that Mr. O. was looking uncomfortable in his seat. He was scowling at Dr. Cronus.

"Are you looking at me funny?" he asked.

"Maybe," the doctor replied.

"Well, don't," said Mr. O. "In fact, don't look at me at all. It's very annoying."

"Not as annoying as you are sometimes," he returned. "Always wanting to be the center of attention."

"Hey, guys, chill," said Selene.

"You can talk," Mr. O. replied to her.

"Me? What have I done? It's you who's full of yourself," said Selene.

"Give me a break. No one's more full of themselves than you when you're full. The whole Earth gets to know about it!"

"So? Being full is part of what I do. I am the Moon, you know."

"Now, now," Joe admonished. "Try to get along."

Selene, Dr. Cronus, and Mr. O. glared at one another.

"Grrr," said Selene.

"Grrr," Mr. O. growled back, and then he picked up a piece of bread from the bread basket and flicked it at her.

"Now stop it," said Joe with a glance at me. "In case Miss Strict Bottom starts up again, because I, for one, want my dinner and my dessert."

"Miss Strict Bottom," Dr. Cronus said, snickering. "Tee-hee. He said *bottom*."

"What's the matter with them?" I whispered to Nessa, who was sitting next to me. "Why are they arguing and acting like five-year-olds?"

"Because of where they've been placed," she whispered back. "The Sun and Saturn are in direct opposition in your chart, and now they are again, sittin' where they've been put by you. There are bound to be arguments. You've put Selene at a strange angle, too."

Oh no, I thought. Of course. It should have been obvious to me. The Sun and Saturn weren't the only ones in opposition. It wasn't long before Joe began to look agitated, too.

"Don't like my seat," he whined.

"Me neither," said Captain John.

And they started with the bread basket, too. First Joe flicked his bread at Selene. She flicked it back. Dr. Cronus threw a chunk of his. It hit Joe on the head, so he joined in. Soon it was a bread fight, with chunks of bread flying through the air, showering crumbs all over the place.

"Fantastic," said Mom. "These guys are so much fun." And *she* joined in.

No, no, I thought. *This isn't how it's supposed to be.* "Rachel, what should I do?"

"As your mom just said, if you can't beat 'em, join 'em," she said, and *she* joined in.

The noise level was rising again, food was flying everywhere, everyone was laughing or yelling insults, and I could hear Mrs. Janson banging on the wall again.

"Les dance again," slurred Selene. "Les all be the ocean." And she got up and started her funny swaying dance. The others didn't need much encouragement to get up and join in.

Captain John looked especially moved. "Yes. Let's be the ocean," he said, and he started waving his arms in the air.

Mr. O. went to put on some music, Nessa yelled, "Conga," and off they went again, in a line, into the kitchen, where Mr. O. found a laundry basket full of underwear. In a second, they each had a pair of Mom's underpants on their heads. This caused great hilarity, especially when Dr. Cronus put on a pair that were pink with purple polka dots. Selene and Mr. O. were on the floor hooting with laughter.

"Stop it, *stop* it!" I cried. "Put everything back in the basket."

But no one listened to me. Underpants on heads,

they got back in their line and conga-ed out the back, once around the yard, and back into the hall.

"We don't get to let our hair down very often," said Nessa as she danced past me, her hair completely loose and wild. "Come on, join in. Let's party."

I felt the knot in my stomach tighten so much that I thought I was going to throw up. I felt my fists clench, too. There was no way I could party feeling like this. I shut the door to the yard behind them, and they conga-ed into the living room. "La la la la la la laaa," they all sang.

And then I heard a scream. I ran to see what was going on.

"Pillow fight," said Captain John, and he whacked Selene on the head. She grabbed one herself and whacked him back.

"Come on," said Rachel, who seemed to be having the time of her life. "I'm really good at this and so are you. Remember, you used to be the pillow-fight champion."

"Yes, come on, Thebe," said Mom as she and Dad picked up pillows, ready to join in.

I felt rooted to the spot. I couldn't believe my eyes. My honored guests, who had arrived only an hour earlier looking so sophisticated, had rolled up their sleeves and were playing and screaming like children. None of them heard the doorbell ring.

Hermie, I thought as I went to answer it. *At last, he's come to save the day.* I opened the door.

It wasn't Hermie.

"Now then, young lady. Are your parents or any adults at home?" asked a serious-looking bald policeman with big teeth. "We've had some complaints."

Selene chose that moment to dance through into the hall. "Herro, occifer," she slurred. "I'm re moon, yunno. D'ya wanna a glass of moon what is is? Majeecan. Mahittan. Moon milk. S'very nice. S'got honey in it. Not supposed to have honey, tee-hee."

Dr. Cronus came after her brandishing a pillow. "Gotcha, gotcha, you naughty little girl," he called as he waved the pillow in the air. Unfortunately, Selene ducked, and Dr. Cronus bashed the policeman over the head. Gently, it must be said, but the officer was not amused.

"I think you'd better come with me, sir," he said.

Dr. Cronus (who still had the underpants on his head) smiled at the policeman and linked arms with him. "Where we going? Some'ere nice? And have you been a good boy today? Done your homework? Good boy, you're very smart. 'ave you gorany honey? Hmm. Les be bees. Buzz buzz buzz just like a busy bee."

At that moment, the other planets emerged from the living room in their conga line, and as they did, I noticed Mom and Dad break off from the end and make a dive for the kitchen, closing the door behind them. Luckily, the policeman was so distracted by what was happening at the front of the house that he didn't notice them disappear.

"Olé, olé, olé, olé," sang the planets as they danced out the front door and down the driveway, where four more policemen were waiting by a large van. One of the policemen opened the doors.

My last sight of our guests was of them being ushered into the back and taken to the police station, leaving Rachel and me staring after them.

"Oops," said Rachel.

Chapter Ten

Paparazzi nightmare

The press went crazy. It was in all of the newspapers the next day. One of them said:

CELEBRITY ASTROLOGER BENJAMIN BATTYE ENTERTAINS THE STARS

Arrests were made at the home of celebrity astrologer Benjamin Battye on Friday night after complaints from the neighbors about noise. Six disorderly people were arrested and kept overnight in jail cells. Staff claimed they'd never seen anything like it, saying that the arrested party were "off their rockers" and "behaving like lunatics." One of them kept saying that she was the Moon, and another claimed to be from the planet Venus, another said he was the king of the gods, and another the king of the sea. The officer in charge said, "I've had idiots in here before thinking that they were Napoleon or Cleopatra, but this takes the cake. Now I've seen it all."

Mr. Battye and his wife, Estella, declined to comment after their guests were taken away, but neighbor Mrs. Janson said that there had been "some very strange comings and goings" at the house in recent weeks.

Other articles weren't as kind.

BENJIE'S PALS ARE TRULY BATTY

A costume party turned ugly when celebrity astrologer Benjamin Battye's guests went truly batty after drinking something named "Aunt Nikkya's fruit punch," which was clearly a code name for something a lot more potent. All were carted off to prison after arguing with police officers and claiming to be from other planets. Selene (the Moon) Luna tried to kiss the officer in charge, and Nessa (Venus) attempted to get Officer Watson and his colleagues to do the conga. Dr. Cronus (Saturn), an esteemed headmaster, hit a policeman and then insisted on wearing a pair of bright pink ladies' underpants on his head and became hysterical if anyone tried to remove them. "A real bunch of lunatics," said Officer Watson. "They should all be locked up for a very long time."

I had gotten out my Zodiaphone the minute after they'd all been taken to the station and texted Hermie. "Urgent. The planets have been arrested. Please help."

But of course he hadn't replied.

"This isn't a joke anymore," I said to Mom the next morning after Dad had gone to the police station with a big wad of cash to use as bail to get our planet friends out.

Mom was lying in bed with the curtains drawn, even though it was ten o'clock. "Still no word from Hermie?" she asked.

"Not one. What's the point of having a guardian if

he's not around when I need him? And I really need him now."

Mom winced. "Not so loud, baby. After that trouble last night, I hardly slept a wink, and I've got a terrible headache."

"I'm not shouting," I replied. "In fact, I'm talking quietly."

"Well, would you mind doing it next door? I need to sleep."

I tiptoed out. She did look tired, and so had Dad this morning, but he'd managed to drag himself out of bed after getting a phone call from the police station saying that if he was willing to post bail and vouch for them, the planet people could be released.

In the meantime, Pat and Yasmin had come home from their sleepover. Both of them were absolutely livid. They had seen the morning papers and blamed me.

"You're a complete idiot, Thebe," said Pat as she showed me the first paper. "*How* could you have let this happen? It will be all around school on Monday. How am I going to explain it? My street cred has been totally destroyed, thanks, or rather, no thanks to you. You are the most stupid idiot on the planet. This whole family is stupid, and now the whole world knows it."

"My sentiments exactly," said Yasmin. "I'm going to call my mom and dad immediately and ask them to get me out of this madhouse as soon as possible. I don't want to stay here another minute, in case what you've all got is contagious!"

Well, if Yasmin goes, at least some good might have come out of last night, I thought as they flounced up to Pat's room and slammed the door behind them. I went to sit on the bottom stair. Outside, the sky was gray and it had begun to rain. *Just like how I feel*, I thought as my eyes filled with tears. I really needed to talk to Rachel, so I got up to get the cordless phone and dialed her number.

"Thebe," she whispered when I'd gotten through. "I'm not allowed to speak to you. Mom's seen the papers and says you and your family are a bad influence."

In the background, I heard her mother. "Is that Thebe Battye? You put down the phone this instant."

"Later," I said. I didn't want to get her into any more trouble. Her mom had looked very angry when she'd come to pick her up and found the house surrounded by police.

Just after I'd put down the phone, I heard a commotion outside. I went over to the window and looked out. Two vans had pulled up outside. Inside were six very grumpy- and disheveled-looking Zodiac people—and Dad.

Minutes later, they trooped in, filed into the living room, and slumped on the sofas and the floor.

"Thebe, get some blankets and water. Lots of it. And strong coffee."

I nodded and set about doing what I was told. After they'd had their coffee, they settled down to sleep, and soon the only sound was that of snoring.

"There's been a storm," said Dad as the doorbell rang, "but I think it will blow over. Get the door, will you?"

I went to the front door and opened it. A bright light flashed in my face.

"Any comment, darlin'?" asked an overweight man with a pale face.

More lights flashed, almost blinding me.

"You Battye's girl?" asked a female voice.

"Were you here last night?" asked a man.

"Any comment?" asked another man.

"Do you think you're from a planet?" asked another, which caused everyone to snicker.

"We need to talk to the chicks who say that they're Venus and the Moon," insisted the pale man. "Exclusive interview with our paper."

"And we want that gorgeous guy who says he's the Sun," said a lady with blond hair and a lot of makeup. "Ask if he'll do a photo shoot in his boxers—especially for the ladies."

I blinked and tried to focus. There must have been around 15, maybe 20 of them.

"Daaaaaaaaaaad," I called.

Dad came into the hall and got what was happening

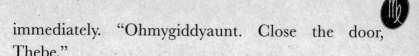

immediately. "Ohmygiddyaunt. Close the door, Thebe."

I closed the door and turned to Dad. "What's going on? Why are they all here?"

"Looks like they've sniffed out that there's more to the story, maybe even realized who they are."

"But people think they're crazy, don't they, not that they're really from other planets? Surely it will blow over."

Dad shook his head. "I hope so, but it might blow our friends' cover while they're down here on Earth. They might all lose their businesses and have to relocate. In the meantime, we have to protect them. This is bad. This could damage our reputation, too. Everything we've worked for. No one will want to buy our merchandise and no one will want to read my columns. We'll be a laughingstock. The batty Battyes. Oh dear, Thebe. You have to go in there and wake them all up, explain the situation, and let's see if we can get them out the back."

It wasn't an easy task waking six hung-over planets.

"Go away," said Nessa. "I need my beauty sleep."

"Noisy, noisy," moaned Selene. "Be *quiet*, noisy person."

"Go and do your homework, please, child," groaned Dr. Cronus.

"Hey! No need for that," I said. "I'm on your side. Look, there are more than a dozen paparazzi outside, and they want to get in and photograph and interview you. Dad says they could blow your cover and destroy our reputation. What are you going to do?"

Dr. Cronus sat up and rubbed his head. I was glad to see that he had taken off the underpants, and besides the bleary eyes, he looked back to his usual serious self. "Hmm. We have a crisis here. Now then, let's think. Okay, Thebe, do you think you've learned your lesson yet?"

"Me! My lesson? What are you talking about? It's you all who have just spent the night in jail, not me."

"Your fault, though," said Nessa. "You organized everything."

I was still reeling from what Dr. Cronus had said, and it seemed very unfair. I felt all the frustration that I'd been holding back about being ignored in my special month bubbling up to the surface. "Listen here, everyone. Okay, so last night was a disaster, but I did my best, truly I did. You're the adults. Tell me what to do."

Dr. Cronus looked at me intently. "Hmm. We need Hermie, don't we? Someone to talk to the press. That's his thing. Communication."

"I tried to call him but didn't get a reply."

"Retrograde," chorused all of the planets, who were beginning to sit up, rub their eyes, and stretch.

Dad appeared at the door. "Come on, everyone," he said. "I've ordered the vans to come back and wait

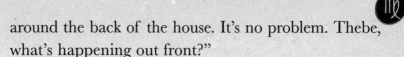

around the back of the house. It's no problem. Thebe, what's happening out front?"

I went over to the window and peeped out. A flash immediately blasted off. "Looks like they're still there."

"Okay, off we go," Dad said, and he handed each of them a scarf as they traipsed past him. "Put these over your heads in case any of the photographers have slipped around the back. You know how sneaky they can be."

Dr. Cronus looked very put out. "This situation is very grave, you know. I hope you all realize that this could be the end of our time here and that we might have to leave."

All of the planets regarded me accusingly.

"Don't look at me. It's not my fault!"

Selene stared at me sadly. "Sometimes you have to know when to stand up and take the blame."

"Come on now," said Dad. "No time to stand around. We need to get you out of here."

"My head hurts," groaned Mr. O., who was looking extremely pale, even with his tan.

"Every bit of me aches," said Captain John Dory.

"Maybe we shouldn't have Zodiac Girls anymore," said Dr. Cronus. "More trouble than they're worth, every one of them."

"At least you'll be remembered," said Mr. O. gloomily, "as the last Zodiac Girl ever."

"End of an era," said Nessa. "We need to go into hiding for a very long time."

They all trooped out the back like they had the weight of the world on their shoulders. I kept watch, and then they were gone. *Maybe forever*, I thought.

Chapter Eleven
An unexpected visitor

I waited for half an hour and then checked out the front again. The press were all still there, leaning on the front wall, some of them smoking cigarettes. I opened the door, and they all snapped to attention.

"You may as well go," I said, "because our guests have left."

"Where've they gone?" asked the pale man.

"Back to their planets probably," I said.

"Oh, she's a funny one," said the blond as she strained to look over my shoulder into the hallway. "Come on, guys, we'll track them down some way or other."

One by one, they began to drift away. I closed the door and went into the kitchen, where I plonked myself down at the table and put my head in my hands. *Nobody understands me or cares. I try so hard to do everything right and make life nice for people, and now it's all gone and backfired.* I wished I'd never been chosen as a Zodiac Girl and I wished I'd never met any of the planets. No good had come from it all. I looked around the kitchen.

The dishes hadn't been washed. Empty glasses were stacked by the sink. Uneaten food still sat in pots and pans. And I knew that the rest of the house was still a mess from last night—crumbs all over the dining room from the bread fight and pillows scattered in the living room from the pillow fight. Mrs. Watson, the housekeeper, never came in on Saturdays, Mom was in bed, and no way would Pat or Yasmin help clean up— it was up to me, as usual. I began to make a mental list of what needed to be done. *I'll start in a minute*, I thought as I picked up a piece of bread from the table and flicked it onto the floor.

Cosmo crawled out of his basket by the door, hopped up onto my knee, and nuzzled my nose as if to say that he understood. Tears dripped down my cheeks and splashed onto the table, while outside the sky opened and rain began to pour. The kitchen lit up as a flash of lightning followed by a rumble of thunder sounded outside.

"Hi there, Cosmo," I said as I nuzzled him back. "I'm a Zodiac Girl this month. Did you know that? It's a very special honor, you know."

"Meow," he replied and put a paw up to my cheek. After hearing a noise in the yard, he suddenly leaped off my lap and ran to the windowsill, hopped up, put up his paws, and looked out.

"What is it?" I asked as I went to join him.

He seemed to be looking at something or someone intently. I soon spotted what it was. A tall, slim man dressed in an electric-blue jumpsuit with silver spiked hair and a lightning bolt painted on his face was standing on our clothesline! He saw Cosmo and me staring, and he waved and smiled and then began to walk along the line as if it was a tightrope.

"He's got to be Uranus," I said to Cosmo. His costume made perfect sense, as both the color and the lightning symbol were commonly associated with that planet. I waved back at him but decided not to venture out. It was absolutely pouring. "I hope his outfit is waterproof," I said to Cosmo as Uri began to move along the line.

It was like watching a circus performer. He walked the line, did a backflip, which made both Cosmo and me gasp, and then he got a small silver umbrella out of a pocket, opened it up, and skipped along to the end of the line. He hopped down onto the grass, went to a backpack in the corner of the yard, and heaved it onto his back. It looked heavy, and he stooped under the weight of it. With bent knees, he did a wobbly comedy walk back over to the line, which he hopped back onto, and then he checked to see that I was still watching him. He stooped even more, grimaced, and looked over at me as if for sympathy. Holding his back with one hand and supporting the backpack with the other, he began to walk across the line again.

"Wow! That must be difficult," I said. "Especially if whatever's in his bag weighs a lot."

"Meow," Cosmo agreed.

Every now and then, Uri checked to see if I was watching, nodded when he saw that I was, and then he'd pull a package out of his backpack and chuck it onto the grass. Then he went back to walking across the clothesline. Then he'd chuck another package. Each time he let a package go, his back straightened up a little. I wasn't sure what to make of it. It was the strangest sight I had ever seen. It was still raining hard, but he didn't seem bothered. As he reached the end of the line, he let a last package go, and as he did, he straightened his back up completely so that once more he was upright and seemed as light as a feather. At the exact moment he tossed the last package aside, the sun came out from behind the clouds, lighting the drops of rain so that they looked like thousands of tiny diamonds, and then he bowed. As he did so, a rainbow appeared in the sky. It was magical.

I opened the back door and clapped.

"You must be Uri," I said.

He bowed again and skipped down off the line. "And you're a Zodiac Girl."

I nodded. "I am, but I'm trying to forget all that now. It hasn't been a very good time for me or any of your friends."

130

"I know. And I'm sorry I didn't make it yesterday to the party. It sounded like fun."

"You wouldn't be sorry if you knew what had happened."

"But I do know. It was part of the plan."

"Plan? What plan? I mean . . . I had a plan, but . . ."

"You're a Zodiac Girl, right?"

"Yes."

"So we all knew what needed to happen, more or less, in your month."

"No. That can't be. I mean, most of the planets took no notice of me . . ."

"That was part of the plan," said Uri, and he looked up at the sky. "Can I step inside? Little wet out here."

Even though I knew who he was, I was sure that Mom wouldn't want me to let a strange man inside the house. "I have to check with Mom first. Wait here."

I ran up the stairs and into her bedroom. Mom was sitting at the window, looking brighter than she had earlier.

"Mom, Uri's here, and he wants to come in for a minute. Is that okay?"

"I saw him in the yard. Marvelous show," she said. "Yes, let him in, but be sure to keep him away from the punch, if there's any left."

"No problem. I poured the rest of it away," I said,

and then I raced back down and let Uri in. Besides his hair, which was now plastered against his head, and rivulets of rain that dripped down his forehead, he didn't look too soaked.

He stepped in and looked around the kitchen, which was done in the bright yellow and orange colors of the Sun. He bent down and stroked Cosmo, who purred at once, and then he sat down at the table. His hair seemed to dry out in an instant. It spiked up all by itself.

"Uri, you don't seem to realize what's been happening here—it can't be part of the plan. The other planets were all off their rockers last night. Totally out of control."

"And isn't that life? Happens sometimes," said Uri with a shrug of his shoulders. "You can't control everything."

I didn't understand. He was making so light of it and it was really serious.

"No. It's all gone wrong. All of it."

Uri sighed. "Thebe, haven't you got it yet?"

"Got what?"

He pointed out the window toward the clothesline and the discarded packages. "What we've all been trying to tell you?"

I felt myself go totally blank. "No. I guess I haven't."

Uri smiled. "To let go, Thebe. That's all. Let go. Sometimes things are out of your control. Sometimes you can control things, sometimes you can't. You have to recognize the difference. Sometimes you have to let go and go with the flow."

I thought back to his show in the rain and how he was letting go of the packages, and as he did, he became lighter. I looked around at the mess on the floor and on the table. And I thought about the past few weeks and all the odd things that had happened.

Suddenly, I *did* get it.

I smiled at Uri, and he smiled back, then got up, bowed, and went out the door into the yard, and a second later, he had disappeared.

I looked around the kitchen and laughed. "Sometimes you just have to let go," I said to Cosmo. I walked into the hall and then the study, where, as always, there were books and papers piled everywhere. "Great," I said. Next I went into the dining room, which looked as if a bomb had hit it. "Fantastic," I said.

Finally, I went into the living room, pushed aside some crumbs on the floor, and then lay down on the sofa. *I think I'll take a little nap*, I thought. *So the house is a mess? So? No biggie. It's the weekend. Time to chill.*

In moments, I was in a lovely deep sleep.

Chapter Twelve
Chaos

Thebe's list of things to do
1) Chill.

"Mom, there's nothing to eat," groaned Pat as she looked in the fridge a few days later.

Cosmo looked down at his empty bowl and then over at me. "Meow-ow," he said.

"Estella, baby, this kitchen is in need of a good clean," said Dad, pinching his nose. "It's beginning to smell." He lifted the lid on the trash can. "Yuck! No wonder! This thing needs to be taken out."

Mom looked around in despair. "I know, the place is a real mess. Let's have a cup of coffee and decide what we're going to do." She looked hopefully over at me, but I didn't budge.

"Good idea," I said. "I'd love a cup of coffee. Thank you very much."

Mom sighed and went over to the coffeemaker. It was empty, as I knew it would be. She sighed again and looked over at me with sad eyes.

Did I care? Not a bit. I was the new me. The chilled me. I was mastering the art of letting go. So far, I'd let go of making my bed in the morning, ordering the groceries, cleaning up, making lists. Okay, so the house was a dump, but I was letting go of that, too.

A gentle thud came from the hall announcing that the mail had arrived. Dad went out to get it and came back moments later, sifting through it. "One for you, Thebe," he said and chucked a postcard at me.

It showed a white beach and turquoise water. I glanced at the sender. "It's from Hermie."

Dad nodded. "That would be right. The retrograde period for Mercury is over the day after tomorrow, so I guessed that he'd be back in contact sometime soon."

"What does it say?" asked Mom.

I read:

"Hello, Thebe,

Hope you've been having a groovy time as a Zodiac Girl. Back soon, will be in touch.

Love,

Hermie.

P. S. Been hanging out with Uncle Norrece over here."

Yet *another* one of my relatives who had been hanging out with one of the planet people! I wasn't going to let it bother me, though. So my guardian had spent a large part of my Zodiac month on a Greek island. Cool.

So he hadn't bothered to try to contact me until now—so what? He was going with the flow, and now so was I. It wasn't up to me to tell him what he should or shouldn't be doing. Nor anyone else for that matter. From now on, I was going to mind my own business and not ever try to organize anyone else's life again.

"Where's the card from?" asked Mom.

I looked at the postmark and stamp. "Greece."

"Of course, that's where Norrece was," said Mom.

"Greece! So that's where Mercury goes when he's retrograde," said Dad. "I'd always wondered."

"And that's nice he's been hanging out with Norrece," said Mom. "He'll be back soon. He and Maggie are getting back together, thanks to the talks they've been having with Selene."

I should have done the same as Hermie. I should have followed his example and just relaxed these past few weeks instead of getting myself into a frenzy, I thought as I put up my feet on the table. "So. What's everyone doing today?" I asked.

"Well, clearly getting things organized around here," said Mom stiffly. "What time's the housekeeper coming? It is her day, isn't it?"

I shrugged. "Dunno. Has anyone contacted her?"

Dad, Mom, and Pat shook their heads.

I glanced at my watch. "She probably came earlier this morning, as always, but . . . did anyone leave the keys in the usual place for her?"

"What's the usual place?" asked Dad.

"I didn't know there was a usual place," said Mom.

"Oh, there is. It's under the Japanese pot on the porch, around the back, for future reference. I usually leave it out for her when I bring the mail in on my way out to school, but since it's school vacation this week, I haven't been out yet."

"Look, Thebe, you've made your point," said Pat. "You ran the household. Fine. But you loved doing it. You know you did. You loved being in control and organizing us all."

"I know. But I've changed. I've realized that I have to let go. Let go of being a control freak. So that's what I'm doing. Letting go of running your lives."

"But why, munchkin?" asked Dad. "You were so good at it."

"Ah, but the planet people showed me that I was trying to control things too much, and actually, it's okay if things get out of hand. It's not the end of the world if things go crazy."

"I'm not sure about that anymore," said Mom as she looked at the pile of unwashed dishes in the sink.

"You have to go with the flow, Mom, and it will all work out just fine. Trust me. Like the other night when our guests got arrested, I thought it was the end, and when the press came the next day, I wanted to die.

I thought I'd ruined it for Zodiac Girls for the rest of eternity—but hey, things worked out, the press moved on to another story and lost interest in us. The planet people are fine with it—in fact, according to Uri, it was all part of their master plan for my month as a Zodiac Girl to teach me a lesson. And my lesson was to let go. So yeah, hey, let's go with the flow."

Pat, Mom, Dad, and Cosmo looked at me unhappily.

I got up, found some cat food at the back of a cupboard, and put it out for Cosmo. I couldn't let him be neglected in any way.

The others were still standing around as if they didn't know what to do with themselves. Finally, Mom sighed and said, "Okay. Pat, you start on the dishes, Benjamin, you can clean the bathroom, and I'll call Mrs. Watson to see if she'll come by again. In the meantime, Thebe, do you think you could do the Internet shopping? Get us some groceries?"

"Maybe later, if I'm not too tired. For now, I'm going to go listen to some music."

I got up and went to my room, where Yasmin was lying on her bed with her headphones on. She barely registered my appearance. Like the rest of the house, the room was a mess, the bed unmade, clothes and socks on the floor. Instinctively, I went to pick up a pair of socks and put them in the laundry basket, but I stopped myself. *Leave it, let go*, I told myself. *Stop being a control freak.*

I lay back on the bed and chuckled to myself. It was all so clear to me now. I hadn't been ignored or abandoned by the planets. From the beginning, they had been trying to tell me to relax. Selene by trying to get me to let out my feelings, Nessa by demonstrating what it was like to have some girlie fun, Mr. O. with his chill-out CD—all of them had been trying to show me how to relax by coming over and hanging out with Dad. I put the CD that Mr. O. had left into the player, put on my headphones, and lay back on my bed to listen. It was nice music, but I felt myself getting fidgety, and my mind kept making lists despite my trying not to. *Old habits die hard*, I told myself. I lay there for another five minutes. Part of me was itching to get up and clean my room. It was like a force inside of me, and I was having a hard time keeping it down. In the end, I couldn't stay there anymore. I knew that if I did, I'd have to give in and clean. I went downstairs to see how Mom and Dad were doing.

"Hi, baby," said Mom as she found a pair of plastic gloves under the sink and put them on.

"Did you have a nice rest?" asked Dad as he put on the Homer Simpson apron that was hanging on the back door and started to empty the trash.

Pat looked at me sulkily as she swept the floor, and then she flounced out and clomped up the stairs.

"I hope you don't think I'm being selfish by not

helping out; it's just that I am trying to make the most of my Zodiac month, and for the first three weeks, I didn't get that they were trying to tell me that I have to let go."

"Baby," said Mom, "we only want what makes you happy. Really we do. And if you want to chill, then you chill, girl."

"Amen to that," said Dad. "Hey, Estella, let's boogie while we work."

Mom's face lit up. "Put on some salsa," she said.

I sat at the table while Dad put a CD into the player, and then they began cleaning up, dancing, and bumping butts along to the music. I wanted to join in so much. I wanted to put on some gloves and get cleaning with them. Nothing made me feel happier than seeing a gleaming counter in the kitchen or smelling the lemon-clean scent of a freshly washed floor, especially when it had been very dirty. I found it so satisfying to make things better. Before my eyes, Mom and Dad were transforming the kitchen back to its usual pristine appearance. *I could start on the living room*, I thought and almost got up to go and get the vacuum from the hall closet. I pushed down the urge and sat on my hands.

I was chilling. I was letting go. Wasn't I? I went back to watching Mom and Dad cleaning and polishing. Dad began sweeping the floor and dancing with the broom.

He missed a little bit of dust under the table. A feeling of frustration began to rise up from deep within me. I tried to push it back, but it kept coming.

"Arrrrggghhhhhhhhhh!"

Mom and Dad stopped what they were doing and turned to stare at me.

"What is it, baby?" asked Mom. "Somethin' bite you?"

"No. *No*. It's hopeless. *I* am hopeless." I got up and stood in front of them as if they were a jury and I was a criminal. "My name is Thebe Battye and I am a control freak. I can't help it. It's who I am. I've tried to fight it. I really have, but I am beyond help, even the help of the stars. And I am sorry, but I have to give in to it." I hung my head. "It's bigger than me. It's bigger than all of us." I took the broom from Dad and began sweeping under the table. "See, Dad, you missed a spot. You weren't doing it *right*!"

Chapter Thirteen

Yasmin

"I guess you'll be going soon?" I asked Yasmin when I found her upstairs later, still lying on her bed. For once, the room was quiet and she didn't even have her headphones on.

She nodded, but she didn't look happy. "Mom's flying back tomorrow, so I'll be going home."

"You okay?" I asked.

"Like you care," she replied.

I went over and sat on the end of her bed. "It will be nice to have my room back—I'm not going to lie—but you're still my cousin and I do care."

Yasmin's eyes filled up with tears, which she quickly brushed away.

"What's the matter?"

"N . . . n . . . nothing," she said, but her eyes were still shining with tears, which she once again attempted to wipe away. "J . . . just . . . waghhhhhhhhhh."

I let her cry for a few moments, but I felt so awkward not doing anything. I tentatively put out my hand and found hers. I was half expecting her to shove it away, but she didn't. She held it fast, and then she sat up, wrapped her arms around me, and sobbed into my shoulder.

"Ohmigod. What's the matter, Yasmin?"

She sobbed for a few more minutes and then sniffed, reached out for a tissue, and blew her nose. "Sorry," she said.

"But I'd have thought you were happy that your mom and dad have gotten back together," I said.

"I am. I really am, but . . . just . . . well . . ."

"What?"

"Oh, everything's wrong in my life."

"In your life? How? Like what?"

"I'm going to miss being here."

"I thought you hated it and thought that we were all crazy."

"Not really. I like it here. I love that all the rooms are done in different colors and styles. I like that your dad dresses like a surfer. My dad is so straight, and our house is cream. And beige. And boring."

"Oh, but it's so clean." (Auntie Maggie was a control freak like me and kept the house spick-and-span.)

"I know that, but it's like living in a hotel, nothing out of place."

"But won't it feel good to be home?"

"In one way, but . . . I love that people are coming and going all the time here, and . . . you never know

143

what's going to happen next."

I was amazed at what she was saying. "I didn't know. I . . ."

"No one knows the real me," she said. "I'm really good at keeping my feelings to myself, besides today, because I feel . . . well . . . I feel terrible."

"You can always come to stay."

"No, I can't. There's not enough room, and I know you haven't liked sharing with me. You made that very clear, and I don't blame you either. I wouldn't want to share my room with me."

"I haven't minded that much, Yasmin," I said, and I attempted a smile. "It's gotten easier."

"How?"

"I realized I had some things to learn."

"You? Like what?"

"Like I don't know everything and I don't have to try to be perfect and I have to chill."

"But that's what's awesome about you. You are so perfect."

"Me? No way. I'm the black sheep of this family. The odd one out."

"No. It's *me* who's the odd one out. Like your whole family is so colorful and interesting. I feel so drab compared to you. Miss Ordinary."

"No. That's *me*. I'm not colorful or interesting."

"Yes, you are. You're amazing. You do everything

so well and are so organized. I so wish I could be like that."

I couldn't believe what I was hearing. This wasn't the Yasmin I knew. "Yasmin, are you on drugs?"

"Course not."

"But I thought you hated me."

"No. Never hated. I envied you and your naturally sunny nature. It made me want to erase you because you showed me up for being such a Miss Misery. Like, you're so thoughtful—you left me oranges and flowers—and in return, I was mean and spiteful."

"I thought you hadn't even noticed."

"I did. And I'm sorry I didn't say so. I was *so* angry when I got here. So mad with my mom and dad for arguing and not even considering how it affected me. It was me who got thrown out of my room and my home. No one asked what I wanted. I was mad at them and I took it out on you, but it wasn't your fault, and I . . . I'm sorry."

"I think I took it out on you, too," I said, and I gave her another hug and laughed.

She pushed me away. "Why are you laughing at me?"

"I'm not laughing at you. Just . . . we're more alike than we realized, and here we are competing for the title of the most boring member of the family. It's . . . very funny if you think about it."

Yasmin regarded me for a moment, and then her

145

face split into a grin. "I suppose it is, but it's definitely me. I get the prize."

"No, *I* do," I said. "I'm the black sheep."

"No, it's me," said Yasmin, but she was smiling.

"Tell you what," I said. "We can be black sheep together."

Yasmin held out her hand. "Deal."

"Deal."

I should have known, I thought as we shook hands. *There was me on my side of the room with all my stuff, and there was her on her side and both of us pushing the other away when we could have been getting along instead.* "And I'm sorry we wasted so much time not getting along. We could have had a nice time together." And then I had the most *amazing* idea.

While Mom, Dad, and Pat got to grips with the rest of the house, Yasmin and I attacked the spare room. We threw a pile of junk onto the front lawn, ready to be taken to the thrift store, took all of the merchandise that Mom wanted to keep and stacked it in the garage, and then we got to work cleaning. I was happy again as I dusted and vacuumed and polished, with Yasmin at my side. When the room was sparkling, we moved in the spare bed and a few of Yasmin's belongings that she didn't need to take home with her. The Saturn room was only a small room, but we made it look cozy and welcoming with some of Mom's posters and zodiac merchandise. Dr. Cronus would be happy with it if he ever made it up the stairs, and Yasmin was absolutely thrilled.

"Voilà," I said. "One spare room that is yours whenever you want to come and stay, because you are and always will be very welcome here."

"Thanks, cuz," said Yasmin, and she flopped onto the bed with a satisfied sigh.

Chapter Fourteen

Hermie's return

"Here he comes," said Dad as we heard the roar of a motorcycle in the distance on Saturday morning.

Mom, Dad, and I stood in the front yard. Mom put an arm around my shoulder and gave me a squeeze. "Now remember, Hermie's about communication, so you make sure you have a good talk with him and tell him all you've been going through."

I nodded. "I'll try." I wasn't sure I could explain to anyone the turmoil that had been going on in my head the past few days. I wasn't sure who I was anymore. How I was supposed to behave. My feelings were all mixed up and nothing seemed to help. My Zodiaphone had started ringing on the exact date that Mercury began to go direct, and all the various planet people had been in touch. Suddenly they all had a lot to say, as if they were making up for the first three weeks.

"Trust in your dreams," Captain John Dory had texted. *Ha!* I thought when I'd read that. My dreams were more like nightmares lately. I'd be cleaning and cleaning a floor, but it remained dirty.

Selene had called to tell me to trust my feelings. Double ha! My feelings were all over the place. One minute I was happy doing my usual thing—making lists, organizing my life—then I'd feel guilty because I was supposed to be letting go. So I'd try to let go and be chilled and not succeed, and *then* I'd feel bad about that. So, trust my feelings? How could I when they were so confused?

Mars sent a note saying, "Make goals, Thebe, that's the thing." Pff. I used to have clear goals and knew exactly where I was going, but now I didn't know what to aim for—to be chilled or to be organized. Like with the ice-skating thing—should I let it go and admit that I was a failure? Or should I give it another try and succeed by letting go on the ice? It was so confusing.

"Enjoy your life," Mr. O. said. *Easy for him to say*, I thought. *Being the Sun, he brightens up everyone's life by simply showing up.*

"Just make sure you do your lessons and hand your homework in on time," said Dr. Cronus in an e-mail. But hadn't trying to be the best at everything been what had gotten me into such a mix-up?

"Eat, drink, be merry," said Joe, the Jupiter man, when he stopped by one night to see Dad. I tried my best to do that. I ate, I drank, but being merry seemed to have escaped me for the time being. I'd never felt so stressed.

Venus also came over one evening and braided my hair into a funky new style with red ribbon threaded through. "At least you can look chilled, even if you're not feeling it," she said, and my new style did look cool. At least she didn't try to tell me what to feel or how to act.

Uri sent me a rubber fish and a sack of potatoes. No note. Dad said that was typical of him, as he is the eccentric member of the group. "One thing you can always expect from Uranus is the unexpected," he said. I put the rubber fish in the sink and wondered if there was some secret message in Uri's gift, just as there had been when he walked along the clothesline throwing off packages. If there was, I couldn't fathom it.

I was hoping that Hermie was going to make sense of it all. His motorcycle slowed down, and he jumped off, took off his helmet, and shook out his hair. He looked tanned and handsome, every inch the Greek god, and I could see that Mrs. Janson was peeking out from behind her curtains. I turned and gave her a wave, and she darted back out of sight.

"Presents from overseas," said Hermie, and he reached into the box on the back of his bike. He handed Dad a bottle of a liqueur called ouzo, and he gave Mom a tiny statue of a Greek god and a bracelet made of shells to give to Pat later. I waited for my turn and hoped that I wasn't going to be forgotten again. I shouldn't have worried because he pulled out what looked like two shoeboxes. "This is for Thebe, my Zodiac Girl," he said.

"What are they?"

"A surprise," he said. "One is for me, one is for you."

I opened my box to find that it was indeed a shoebox, but inside there weren't any shoes—there was a pair of beautiful white ice skates. I gave them straight back. "No," I said. "I can't skate, and as part of my letting go of trying to be the best at everything, I am admitting it here, in public."

Hermie looked disappointed that I didn't want his gift.

"But what about that party?" asked Dad. "You're still going to come to that, aren't you?"

"I might come and just watch," I said, but even as I said it, I knew that if I went and all the others were skating and I wasn't, I was going to go right back to feeling like the boring member of the Battye family.

Hermie regarded me closely. "Come with me and I'll take care of you."

"Yes. Why don't you go, baby?" Mom said. "And Dad and I will come to join you."

"I could give you a ride on my bike," said Hermie. "I have a spare helmet."

"I can't," I said. "I can't skate, and I've never been on the back of a bike."

"You just hold on and let go," said Hermie.

151

"That's contradictory. How can you hold on and let go at the same time?"

"One's physical, the other's mental. Give it a try."

I didn't want to appear ungrateful or difficult. "Okay," I said. "I'll come on the bike, but I'm not skating."

Hermie gave me a helmet that I put on, and then Mom and Dad helped me up behind him onto the bike. "Hold on, let go," said Dad, laughing.

It's all right for him, I thought. *He'll be coming in a nice, safe car.*

Hermie started up the bike, and va voom, we were off, whizzing down the street. I clung onto Hermie's waist and shut my eyes tight. Air whooshed past, making a roar in my ears. After a few minutes, I dared to look to my left. Our neighboring houses were a blur, and I felt as if I'd left my stomach back at home. I closed my eyes again.

"You okay back there?" asked Hermie.

"Errfff," I called back and clung on even tighter. *Okay, I'm doing the holding-on part*, I thought. *That seems to be going all right—now I need to do the letting-go part.* "Let go, let go, let go," I whispered to myself. I opened my eyes again. I stared at Hermie's back. I didn't dare look around in case I threw up. I decided to close my eyes again. *One thing at a time*, I told myself. I could hold on, but letting go was still an alien concept.

Ten minutes or so later, we slowed down and stopped. I hopped off, and Hermie took the bike to the parking-lot area while I waited for him on the steps and tried to stop shaking. Mom and Dad weren't far behind; they parked alongside the bike and got out of the car with a cheery wave.

Once inside the entrance to the rink, Mom and Dad went to rent skates, while I went with Hermie into the skating area. It was empty.

"Where are all the skaters?" I asked.

"They'll be here this afternoon," said Hermie. "We've got exclusive use of the place for the rest of the morning. My gift to you for having had a rough first three weeks of your Zodiac month."

"I'm still not skating," I said. "I . . . I'm not being difficult. I just can't." The thought of it terrified me.

"We'll take it one step at a time," Hermie said, and he slipped off his sneakers, sat down, and put on his skates. "Watch me first."

In a flash, he was up and on the ice. He was wonderful to watch as he moved with the grace of a dancer and the speed of an athlete.

"Almost as if he has winged feet," said Dad as he came up behind me.

"Well, he would, wouldn't he? Being Mercury," said Mom, coming to join us.

Mom, Dad, and I watched in awe as he sped around

the ice, spun around, skated on one foot, the other held up, skipped, leaped, and then held positions as if he was a statue. After a display worthy of the best professional skater, he came back over to where I was and pointed at the skates. "Ready to give it a shot?"

I laughed, or rather snorted. "I don't think so."

"Just give it a try," said Mom. "We'll all hold one another up."

Dad nodded encouragingly.

The three of them stood and looked at me with pleading eyes.

Mom started doing a silly dance, walking onto the ice and beckoning me with her arms. "Thebe, Thebe Battye," she said in a silly, dreamy voice that I supposed was meant to sound like she was trying to hypnotize me or put me into a trance. "Come onto the ice, come onto the ice."

Dad took his cue from her and joined in, doing the same beckon and silly voice. "Come onto the ice."

"Okay. Okay. If only to get you to be quiet and stop being so embarrassing." I gave in and sat down to put on the skates. "But I'm not going far."

Dad gave me the thumbs-up. "That's my girl."

When I had the skates on, Dad and Hermie helped me to my feet, and I walked to the rink like I had bricks on my feet. "Don't let go," I begged.

"We won't," Dad promised.

As soon as we got onto the ice, I let go of Hermie and grabbed the surrounding wall with my left hand. I hadn't even tried to skate, but already my feet felt clumsy and my knees were giving way.

"Now can you see?" I asked. "I am not going to be able to do this. I've tried, I really have, and I can't."

Hermie stood by my left side. "Give me your hand," he said.

I shook my head. "Can't."

"We've got you," said Dad. "You can let go."

I shook my head again. In the meantime, Mom had skated off into the middle of the ice. She lacked the grace that Hermie had and wobbled as she skated, but she was staying up. Since she was wearing a pink sweatsuit, she resembled a stick of cotton candy, and I couldn't help but smile.

Dad giggled, too. "If your mother can do it, you can," he said.

I took a deep breath and gave Hermie my hand again, and between Dad and him, they pulled me out into the middle of the ice.

"I don't like it," I said as we began to move across. "I don't want to do it." I wanted to go home to something familiar and do something I knew I was good at.

"Just a couple of circuits," said Hermie. "Then if you really want to, we're out of here."

I felt a knot grow in my stomach as they pulled me

along between them. On the second circle of the rink, I began to feel that I could trust them and relaxed a little.

"That's it," called Mom. "See, baby, you can do it."

And then my knees buckled and I lost my balance, which caused Dad to wobble, and then, like dominoes, we all went over. One, two, three, onto our backs.

"Ouch," I cried as my bottom hit the ice.

Hermie was up in a flash and offered me a hand up.

"Argh," groaned Dad. "You okay, munchkin?"

To my surprise, I was. I'd fallen. I'd survived. I looked at my hands. No one had skated over my fingers.

At that moment, music blasted out from the speakers that were positioned on the ceiling—great disco music with a good beat. The lights went up, and soon after, Mr. O. appeared at the entrance to the rink. He was looking very dapper in a white tracksuit with a silver stripe up the side. He skated out onto the rink and, like Hermie, was a natural. He skated around once and then did an amazing circular jump.

"Ah, yes, the half loop," said Hermie as he watched him. "Full rotation jump with a loop entry and—yes!—landing on the back inside edge of the opposite foot. Marvelous." He clapped, Mr. O. bowed, and then Hermie leaned over to me. "He's such a showoff, isn't he? Thinks he's the center of the universe."

I laughed. "Technically, I guess he is, being the Sun and all," I said, but I knew what Hermie meant.

Mr. O. skated over to join us, and he and Hermie helped me and Dad up onto our feet, and I had another skate around the rink with Mr. O. on one side and Hermie on the other. This time, we didn't fall over, and for a few moments, with the music blasting, I felt as if I was flying. *Totally cosmic*, I thought, when for a moment I glanced to either side of me and realized who was supporting me. Skating along with the Sun and Mercury isn't your average Saturday morning. Once around again and the sensation got stronger. And then I realized that Mr. O. had let go and gone off to join Mom and Dad and it was only Hermie who was holding one of my hands.

"No! Argh!" I cried as I panicked, lost my balance, and fell backward again. *The-whump.* "Ouch."

Mom and Dad came over again in an instant. "You okay? You had enough?"

I got up, rubbed my rear end, and decided that I was okay. And I wanted to do it again. This time, Mom and Hermie took me around. After a while, I started to sense that I had my balance. I could feel it—I just had to get my weight distributed right. "You can let go, Mom, but keep holding me, Hermie, please."

Mom let go and skated off, and Hermie and I whizzed off on our own. "You're doing really well," he said as he slowed down the pace a little. "I was told that you catch on to things fast, and you're doing fantastic.

Now strike out to the left, that's it, now the right. Keep the balance. You're doing just fine."

Now that I had him to myself for a few moments, I decided to take the opportunity to tell him what I'd been going through. "I haven't felt fine lately," I said. "In fact, I've never felt so mixed up, like I don't know who I am anymore."

"Who really does?" said Hermie as he led us to the wall for a break. We stood, caught our breath, and watched the others, who seemed to be having a good time in the center. "Finding out who you are is a lifetime's lesson. You're changing and growing all the time. Finding out who you are is an ever-evolving process."

I thought about that for a moment. "I guess. But what I was trying to say is that I don't know what I was supposed to get from this month. I don't know what I was supposed to do as a Zodiac Girl."

Hermie nodded. "Actually, you didn't, or don't, have to do anything. It's all taken care of, but it can be tough when your guardian isn't around to explain things—but as Uri said to you, me being away was all part of the plan. It was no coincidence that your Zodiac month fell when I was on vacation, I mean, ahem . . . retrograde. Nothing could have been more perfect for you at this time for what you needed to experience."

"*Perfect?* But it was a crazy plan."

Hermie chuckled. "Nope. It's all unfolding exactly as it should. See, sometimes it's not what life throws at you that makes your life—it's how you react to it."

"What? Like if life throws lemons, make lemonade?" I asked, quoting one of Auntie Francelle's favorite expressions.

"Something like that. You always have a choice—be miserable or make the most of things."

"But isn't that what I was doing in my own way, making the best of things? Organizing my crazy family, making my lists. I knew where I was with them."

Hermie nodded. "The upside of being a Virgo is that you can be tremendously well organized and efficient. The downside is that you can be—"

"Controlling and obsessive," I finished for him.

He grinned. "Yep."

I remembered what Mom had said about Hermie being the master of communication, so I decided to tell him my worst fears. "And there's something else . . ."

"What's that?"

"I . . . I was worried that the reason none of the planet people, and even you, weren't interested in me is because I am so boring. The black sheep of the Battye family. The rest of them are so glamorous and interesting."

"Thebe," said Hermie, "you are interesting, too. Don't you know that? Your chart says that you have the potential to do great things. Haven't you ever wondered why you're so good at organizing stuff?"

"I just do what comes naturally. It's nothing special."

"Believe me, Thebe, it is. You have what it takes to be a very high achiever. Already, you're an A student—but this is the worry for people like you. You can burn out. You work, work, work—that's why if you can get what we're trying to tell you this month, your Zodiac month, you'll be set up for a lifetime. To be the best, you have to find balance in your life. Understand that and you will go to the top and stay there."

"You really think so?"

"It's all there in your chart. You're a top-class girl," he said, and then he laughed. "You just have to be careful that you don't burn out or let your batteries get flat. Now. Want to see me go retrograde?" He began to back away.

"Noooo," I called, but he was gone, skating backward. He did a lap of the ice rink in reverse and then returned. "Now, want to see me go forward?" And off he went, skating ahead as normal. I watched and laughed. After another lap, he came back. "Ready to try on your own?"

What he'd said to me had made me feel so good that I felt like I could take on the world. I was a top-class girl. Possibly a high achiever. Not boring. I nodded. "But hang onto me until I'm ready," I said.

Hand in hand, we skated out onto the ice. The music was still blasting out.

"I think I can do it," I told him after we'd skated for a few minutes.

"Sure?"

I nodded.

"Find your balance," he said.

I smiled back at him. "I'll try."

He let go, and off I skated, on my own. *Balance and let go,* I thought as I sailed off. *Balance and let go.* It felt wonderful. Flying along to the music, I began to think about which foot went where and what my arms should be doing. Immediately, my knees wobbled, and down I went. Once again, Mom and Dad skated over, their faces full of concern.

"I'm okay," I said. "And I can do it! Almost."

They helped me to my feet, and together we skated to the wall.

Mr. O. and Hermie were skating together, and once again, I marveled at their grace.

"You have a good chat with Hermie?" asked Mom.

"I did, and I think I understand what they've been trying to tell me," I said.

"What's that, munchkin?" asked Dad.

"I can be who I am. I can be me, Thebe, who likes to be in control—I just have to know when to let go. Hold on, let go, and it's all about balance."

"Sounds like good advice." Mom smiled back.

I felt the knot that had been in my stomach for the past few weeks begin to unravel, and I was lighter. It was going to be okay. Mercury going retrograde hadn't been the disaster that I'd imagined and my Zodiac month hadn't been a waste of time. I'd gotten it. It had taken some time, but I'd gotten there in the end.

Hermie looked over at me from the center of the rink and beckoned me over. I gave him the thumbs-up. I could do it. It was all a question of balance. And if I lost it, so what? I could always get up and try again. Things didn't have to be perfect all the time. And neither did I.

I pushed off from the wall and skated toward him.

A week later, it was the night of celebrity ice skater Janet Johnson's party. Lots of press were there, and Dad had invited the whole family. Auntie Francelle, Auntie Nikkya, Auntie Maggie and Uncle Norrece (who were back together again), Yasmin, Pat, Rachel—and Hermie. At first there was a freestyle skate off for everyone, and I felt so relieved to be able to join in and not be the only one from our group out on the benches watching.

Around an hour into the evening, Janet did a solo performance, and it was breathtaking to watch her as she appeared to fly on the ice. She really was the bee's knees, almost as good as Hermie and Mr. O., but not quite. The audience loved her and cheered and cheered, and then she went off to have her picture taken for the papers.

After that, various guests got up and did turns while we watched, and it was soon after that Hermie came up behind me. "Your turn," he said. "Ready?"

I gulped and then nodded. "Ready."

"She wants to see the whole Battye family skate," he said, and I looked over to see that Mom, Dad, and Pat had on their skates and were beckoning me onto the ice.

I can do this, I thought as a wave of panic flooded through me. *I can do this*. Hermie had given us some practice sessions over the week and shown us a simple routine that looked good but wasn't too challenging. I stood up, put my skates back on, and went to join them.

"Nervous?" asked Dad.

I nodded, and he took my hand and squeezed it. "Me, too, but we'll help one another."

Mom gave me an encouraging smile, and the four of us held hands and skated out into the center of the ice.

"And now for Benjamin Battye, celebrity astrologer, and his family," said a man standing by a microphone at the side of the rink.

A spotlight beamed on us, music with a disco beat started up, and we went into our routine. Shimmy, shake, and skate. It was only four minutes around the rink, a little rotation, part reverse, and then we bowed. The rink erupted in applause, and I looked around at the guests watching us and felt a warm glow of happiness. I felt like a star. For once, I was there with Mom, Dad, and Pat—*me*, Thebe Battye, at the center of attention along with them, not standing in the shadows watching as one of them took center stage. Yasmin was grinning and waving, and I spotted Hermie next to her in the bleachers. He nodded and gave me the thumbs-up. I gave him the thumbs-up back and promptly fell on my bottom.

The Virgo Files

Characteristics, Facts, and Fun

August 24th—September 23rd

Patient, kind, and well-organized, Virgos are wonderful listeners and calm in a crisis, making them the perfect sign to have as a close friend. They are often shy, but don't be fooled—Virgos can stand up for themselves if they need to!

Don't invite a Virgo to your house if you have a messy bedroom—they are often obsessively neat and can't stand a mess. These girls want to look perfect and can be materialistic. They like to have the best clothes, but they are unlikely to lend you anything in case you ruin it!

Element:	Earth
Color:	Blue
Birthstone:	Sapphire
Animal:	Cat
Lucky day:	Wednesday
Planet:	Mercury

Virgo's best friends are likely to be:
Cancer
Capricorn
Taurus

Virgo's enemies are likely to be:
Aries
Leo
Libra

A Virgo's idea of heaven would be:
A nice long walk in the country followed by a healthy meal.

A Virgo would go crazy if:
They had to spend time in a pigsty!

Famous Virgos:
Beyoncé
Cameron Diaz
Michael Jackson
Keanu Reeves
Nicole Richie

Here's the first chapter of another fantastic
Zodiac Girls story, **Discount Diva**.

Chapter One

The Crazy Maisies

I wish, I wish, I wish I could go, I thought when our teacher Miss Creighton first made the announcement.

". . . I will be taking names from all you eighth-grade girls in the next week," she continued. "All those who want to go must register before the end of May, which only gives you two weeks."

A school trip to Venice. Two weeks in sunny Italy. I wanted to go more than anything, ever, since the beginning of eternity and even before that.

"You going to put your name down, Tori?" asked Georgie when the bell rang and we headed out of the classroom for our lunch break.

I shrugged my shoulders as if I didn't really care. "Maybe," I said.

"I definitely am," said Megan, catching up with us and linking arms. "Mom said I could go on the next

i

school trip, wherever it was."

"Me, too," said Hannah, linking arms with Megan.

"Me, too," said Georgie. "Which means *you have* to come, Tori. It wouldn't be the same without you. The Crazy Maisies hit Europe."

Me, Hannah, Megan, and Georgie. We called ourselves the Crazy Maisies. My mom used to call me that when I was little and acting silly. Me and my friends act silly a lot, hence the name.

"Venice isn't *that* great," I said. "Too many tourists. Florence is much more interesting." Ha. Like I'd been to either of them. Not. But I had heard my well-traveled Aunt Phoebe saying that Venice was so full of tourists these days that you could hardly move.

"You *have* to come," said Hannah. "And so what if there are loads of tourists? We'll be four of them!"

"Yeah," said Georgie. "Italy, here we come!"

I felt a sinking feeling in my stomach. I was *so* going to miss out, but I could never tell them the real reason why I couldn't go.

"Si, signora, pasta, cappuccino, tiramisu," I said, trying to remember all the Italianish words that I had ever heard and to distract them from trying to persuade me to go. I'd have to think up some excuse that they'd all buy later.

"Linguine, Botticelli, spaghetti . . ." Megan joined in.

"Da Vinci, Madonna, pizzeria, Roma," said Hannah.

Then they started singing a song that we'd done in music class last quarter. We'd had a substitute teacher who had us singing songs from around the globe. "Trying to broaden your horizons," he said as he taught us folk songs from Italy to Iceland. By the end of the quarter, however, I think he was glad to broaden his horizons and move on to another school where the students weren't tone-deaf.

"When the moon hits your eye like a big pizza pie, that's *amore* . . ." my friends chorused off-key and in terrible Italian accents.

A few ninth-grade girls sloped past and looked at us as if we were crazy. I play-acted that I wasn't with them, but Georgie dragged me back, and Hannah and Megan got down on their knees, put their hands on their hearts, and continued hollering away at the tops of their voices.

Crazy. They all are. And they'll have a great time in Venice, that's for sure. Another thing that was for sure was that no way would I be going with them. Not a hope in heck.

During break, we went out into the playground, found a bench on the sunny side, and did each other's hair. When we first met, only Georgie, out of the four of us, had long hair. After a short time hanging out together, we all decided to grow our hair to the same length so that we could play hairdresser, and long hair is best for experimenting with. Georgie and Meg are blond, although Megan's hair is thicker and golden blond, while Georgie's is fine white-blond. Hannah and I have ordinary brown hair, although Hannah has had chestnut highlights put in hers lately. It looks totally cool. I'd love to have highlights, but that's another thing to add to the "not going to happen unless Mom wins the lottery" list.

I think Georgie's the prettiest of the four of us, although Megan and Hannah are good-looking in their own ways too. Hannah could pass for being Mexican. She has olive skin and amazing dark brown eyes, which look enormous when she puts on makeup, and Megan has a sweet face, cornflower-blue eyes, and a tiny nose like a doll. Out of all of us, boys mostly pay attention to Georgie and me, though. Hannah and Megan say it's because I'm pretty too, but sometimes I wonder if the main reason that boys talk to me is to get in with Georgie.

I'm not huge in the confidence department. Some days I can look okay—I know I can—but I could look lots better if I got my hair done professionally and bought some fab new clothes and makeup, but I doubt if that's going to happen anytime soon. Reason being, my family is broke and a half, so it's hard trying to keep up on the appearance front. Most of my clothes come from secondhand stores, but I worry that my friends will find out. At school, girls who don't wear the latest designer clothes get called Discount Divas because their clothes don't have recognizable labels. Megan, Georgie, and Hannah have no idea that I'm Queen Discount Diva.

"I think we should go for a really sophisticated look when we're in Venice," said Megan as she pulled back Georgie's hair and began to braid it.

"No. I think we should wear it loose," said Hannah.

"Yeah," said Georgie. "Loose and romantic-looking. There might be some cute Italian boys to flirt with."

Oh, no! Boys! Italian boys. I hadn't thought of that. What if one of my friends got a boyfriend and I wasn't there to share it all with them? What if all *three* of them got boyfriends and had their first kiss? It might happen. I've heard that Italy is a really romantic place. *Romeo and Juliet* happened over there, and they were *way* loved up. I've also heard that Italian boys are very hot-blooded. (I'm not totally sure what that means and whether they really do have hotter blood than us on account of living in a warmer climate. Whatever.) Apparently they are more forward than American boys, who mostly seem more interested in computers than they do in girls. Anyway, I would be left so far behind in the game of love. I'd be like Cinderella left at home while everyone else went to the ball. Eek! That would be freaking *tragic*. The Crazy Maisies do everything new together—that way we can talk about it all and see how we all feel.

"Ow," said Hannah with a wince as I brushed her hair up into a ponytail. "You're hurting me."

"Sorry," I said and made myself brush more gently. I didn't mean to take my frustration out on her, but all the talk for the next few weeks would be about the trip. And then they'd go, and I'd be by myself. And then they'd come back, and all the talk would be about the trip again. And I'd have nothing to say because I wouldn't have been there. I'd be left out. It would be awful.

Luckily, Megan changed the subject and began making plans for the weekend. A new comedy was playing at the local movie theater. Of course, everyone was up for seeing it.

"Cool!" said Georgie. "And we could go for a snack afterward."

Megan and Hannah nodded enthusiastically. "Lots of those spicy, cheesy taco thingies. I loooove them."

"Ice cream for me," said Georgie. "Pistachio with . . . strawberry."

"Pecan fudge is my fave," I joined in.

"We'll have to do the early show, around six o'clock, or Mom won't be able to pick me up," said Hannah.

I did a quick calculation as they were discussing how they were going to get there and back and what they were going to eat. I'd need money for the movie. Snack. Coke. Nope. No way could I do it on my allowance money. I get around one fourth of what my friends get, and some weeks when things are really tight, Mom can't give us anything at all—us being me, my older sister, Andrea, and my two brothers, William and Daniel. I took a deep breath and got ready to apply my usual philosophy: when the going gets tough, the tough bluff it.

"I can't make it tonight. Mom got me and Dan and Will tickets for the Cyber Queens gig."

"The Cyber Queens? Wow! You *lucky* thing!" said Georgie.

"You've kept quiet about that this week," said Megan. "Those tickets are like the hottest in town."

Hannah playfully punched my arm. "Yeah. Why didn't you tell us?"

"Mom only told us last night. It was a surprise for when we got home."

"A surprise? That's *so* cool," said Georgie. "Your mom is so awesome. I wish my mom did stuff like that. I bet my mom hasn't even *heard* of the Cyber Queens. Can she get the rest of us tickets?"

"Don't think so," I replied. "I think she got the last ones."

"Take your digital camera," said Hannah. "Take lots of pictures to show us."

"Sure," I said.

I felt guilty when the bell rang for afternoon classes. Not only did I not have tickets for the Cyber Queens, but I don't have a digital camera either, even though I'd told everyone that my grandma had gotten me one as an early birthday present. I lied. I don't really like doing it, but sometimes it's necessary. I have to make things up so that they don't think that I'm a total loser. My friends have rich parents who buy them all the latest stuff: iPods, cell phones with cameras, computer games, designer clothes. They've all got their own TVs *and* their own computers in their bedrooms. I don't even have my own bedroom. Not even my own bed. Not really. I have to share a room and a bunk bed with my sister, Andrea. Sometimes I sleep on the downstairs sofa just to get a bit of space, although even then I have to share it—with our cats, Midnight and Meatloaf. (My brother Will named them. Midnight's black, and Meatloaf is a dark tabby.)

Anyway, my friends would surely dump me if they knew the truth about my situation and how poor we really are compared to them. When we first all started hanging out together as a group at the beginning of this year, to dissuade them from coming over, I told them that our house was being redecorated from top to bottom—kitchen, bathroom, the whole thing. I keep telling the girls that we're having "nightmares" with the workers, who keep letting us down. It's an expression that I've heard their parents use a million times.

So far, they haven't been over a lot, but when they have been, my excuses have worked, because the fact is, our house does look like it's in the middle of being redecorated. The walls are patchy with daubs of paint here and there where we decided to try out some paint samples but there wasn't enough cash to buy the paint. There are no carpets on the stairs. The carpets that are down on the floor are worn. There are floorboards up here and there. The whole place looks like it needs to be ripped out and redone from top to toe, so my story has never met with any questions.

Sometimes I think that Georgie may have caught on, but she's never come out and said anything, not yet anyway. It can be stressful on the rare occasions when the girls do come over since I'm afraid that Andrea, Will, or Dan might blow my cover. Instead, I try and make sure that we hang out at Megan, Hannah, or Georgie's houses. I tell them that the floor's up again or the water's off or something. They're so sympathetic that I feel rotten, especially since Georgie seems to like coming to our house, and she always brings something with her, like some fab muffins or expensive chocolate cookies or elderflower juice (my fave).

All my friends are kind. They invite me to sleep over at their houses when I lay on the construction nightmare scenario really thick—like last week I said that a plumber had caused a burst pipe and there was water everywhere. I like going to Georgie's place the best. It's awesome. They have five bedrooms at her house for just her and her mom. *Five*. And seeing as Georgie is an only child, that means that they have three spare. *Three*. I wish I could go and live with her sometimes, although I know deep down that I'd miss my family and especially the cats. Her house is like a palace compared to where I live; I feel like a princess when I'm there, and her mom never interferes with her life. Not like my house. No privacy there. Not even in the bathroom, as there is always someone knocking on the door telling whoever is in there to hurry up.

Some days, like today, being poor stinks. It is Friday. May 12th. The whole world would be out enjoying the early summer sun this evening. Certainly half of our school would be. Everyone down at the local theater to watch a movie and hang out. Some of the older girls from our school would also be there, showing off the fab new outfits they'd just got. There would probably even be some boys there from Marborough High down the road. And I'd have to miss out on the whole outing because I haven't got enough money to go.

As we got up to go back into school, there was a sudden blast of wind, blowing up dust and debris from the playground.

"Whoa," said Georgie as her skirt billowed up. "Where's that come from?"

"Dunno," said Meg, "but let's run."

In an instant, more papers and candy wrappers began to blow in a mini tornado around the playground as the kids headed back inside. A piece of paper flew toward me and stuck to my hand. I flicked it off, but it fluttered back again, and we all laughed, because after I brushed it off for the second time, it seemed to follow me as we headed back to the classroom. It was dancing along behind me, and just before I reached the door, it blew right up until it covered my face so that I couldn't see.

"Bleurgh," I blustered as I pulled it away from my eyes.

"Maybe it's meant for you," said Megan, taking the paper away from me. "Let's see what it is."

"Yeah, right," I said. "Maybe it's a message from a fairy." I was teasing her because last year she was into fairies and angels, and her bedroom was covered with posters of them.

"What does it say?" asked Hannah.

Megan scanned the paper. "Dear Tori, You are to go to the bluebell dell at midnight on Friday night . . ."

I punched her arm playfully. I knew she was making that up. "What does it really say?"

"It looks like some sort of promotion-type thing," she replied. "Um . . . advertising local businesses kind of thing. A beauty salon in Osbury. A café/deli. An astrology website. Stuff like that."

"I'll chuck it," I said and took it to put it in the garbage can in the corner of the playground. As I threw it away, there was a flash of lightning and then a rumble of thunder in the distance. I glanced up. The sky had darkened, threatening sudden rain, so I raced back to join the others at the door.

"The fairies are angry that you threw away their business promotion," joked Georgie.

"Yeah, right. Fairies and elves are alive and well and have taken over Osbury." I laughed back.

Seconds later, the sky opened, and rain pelted down, so we darted inside as quick as we could.

"Phew," I said as we raced along the corridors. "Just made it."

As we settled into class, our teacher, Miss Wilkins, was busy closing the windows that had been open earlier in the morning. The rain continued pouring down, and the wind was still whipping up debris outside. As she reached the last window at the back of the class near my desk, a piece of paper blew in. It sailed right across the classroom and landed *plonk* in front of me.

Meg, Hannah, and Georgie turned to look. I glanced down. It was the same piece of paper that had been following me in the playground! Beauty salon, deli, astrology website . . .

Maybe Megan was right and there were fairies and guardian angels out there. Maybe this was a message from one of them in code or something. *Yeah. And I'm the richest girl in the world*, I thought. However, the paper arriving in front of me did make me wonder. I didn't believe in fairyland like Meg did, but I *did* believe that some things are meant to be. Like fate. Or destiny. And *this* was a coincidence. I couldn't deny that. Maybe it *was* meant for me. I was about to put the paper in my backpack to look at it more carefully later when Miss Wilkins closed the last window and turned back to the class. As she did, she saw the paper that had landed on my desk.

"That garbage is blowing everywhere!" she said as she picked it up, ripped it into tiny pieces, and took it to the front of the room, where she threw it away. "Such a nuisance."

Oh, no, I thought as I watched her do it. *There goes the message about my destiny—straight into the trash!*